DON'T
LOOK
BACK

D1596322

BOOKS BY D.K. HOOD

D.K. HOOD

DON'T LOOK BACK

bookouture

Published by Bookouture in 2022

An imprint of Storyfire Ltd.
Carmelite House
50 Victoria Embankment
London EC4Y 0DZ

www.bookouture.com

Copyright © D.K. Hood, 2022

D.K. Hood has asserted her right to be identified as the author of this work.

All rights reserved. No part of this publication may be reproduced, stored in any retrieval system, or transmitted, in any form or by any means, electronic, mechanical, photocopying, recording or otherwise, without the prior written permission of the publishers.

ISBN: 978-1-80314-179-4
eBook ISBN: 978-1-80314-180-0

This book is a work of fiction. Names, characters, businesses, organizations, places and events other than those clearly in the public domain, are either the product of the author's imagination or are used fictitiously. Any resemblance to actual persons, living or dead, events or locales is entirely coincidental.

This story is for those who have been hurt, trampled, bullied, battered, or used and have had the courage to move forward—I salute you.

PROLOGUE

Darkness surrounded Sheriff Jenna Alton as she pressed her back against the cold brick wall. Heart pounding, she reached for her weapon to find nothing at her side, no Glock, no flashlight or phone. Empty pockets lay flat and the thin material was no barrier to the cold seeping into her flesh. Heart hammering, she edged along the alleyway. The stink of garbage from the overflowing dumpsters caught in her throat like sour milk. Terror claimed her, closing her airways and making it hard to breathe, but she must move on. Legs heavy, she dragged them, step by step to the dumpster, and climbing onto an upturned trash can, peered inside. A young girl, eyes fixed in death, her neck a bloody smile, lay tossed out with the garbage. Horrified, Jenna jumped down and pressed her fist to her mouth to contain the threatening sob. She would be next if she didn't get to safety. Keeping to the shadows, she reached the end of the alleyway, and peered at the empty blacktop. Stores lined the road and their glass façades stared back at her like the unforgiving blackened sockets in a skull.

Grasping at the moss-covered red brick wall, she edged forward. Ahead, shadows crept toward her. The black fingers seemed to grow longer and more threatening with each step. The unfamiliar straight road vanished into a thick mist. Nothing seemed right. Where was she? What was this place? She had to keep moving. An obvious threat loomed like an entity menacing her in the darkness. Close by, running footsteps echoed down the sidewalk. They were coming for her and she couldn't suck in enough air to breathe, let alone run. She glanced down at her sticky hands and gasped at the blood dripping from her fingers. What had happened?

One thing was for sure, she had to run. Lifting her knees, she made it across the blacktop. Gunshots rang out. Bullets slammed into the wall beside her head, sending slithers of brick deep into her tender flesh. Running past the storefronts, she turned to see a figure soaked in blood. She swallowed hard. The reflection in the window wasn't her. Blonde hair framed a once familiar face and panic gripped her. This couldn't be happening. The face staring back at her was the woman she'd left behind a lifetime ago: DEA Agent Avril Parker.

Jenna screamed and her throat unclogged. The next moment, someone had her by the arms, shaking her. She screamed again. It was her time to die.

"Jenna. Open your eyes."

The familiar voice dragged her from the horror. She blinked, immediately recognizing the person beside her. Her close friend and second in command, Deputy David Kane. "Dave?"

"Yeah." He rubbed her arms. "You had another nightmare." He glanced at the clock. "It's almost five. I'll make coffee. Was it the same dream again?"

Jenna pushed her raven hair from her face and nodded. "Yeah. I need to see a shrink. I'm losing my mind."

"You know that's not an option." Kane stood and stretched. "I figure it's time to tell me the truth about what happened during your last assignment. What exactly made the US

Marshals change your face and hide you here in plain sight? Once you have it off your chest, the nightmares will end or I'll be in the dream with you, and you know darn well I'll never allow anything to happen to you."

Jenna chewed on her fingers and then nodded. She trusted him implicitly. "Okay, but this is going to take some time, and you're not going to like what I have to tell you."

ONE

FOUR YEARS AGO

Carlos Vineyard, California

DEA Agent Avril Parker flattened her back against the wall and peeked around the corner of the building. Ahead, almost hidden in the shadows, guards patrolled the area with M4A1 Carbines. It seemed overkill for the protection of a shipment of wine. After overhearing a fragment of conversation about tightening security and hearing trucks arriving in the middle of the night over the last three days, she'd decided to find out what was happening. It might be the breakthrough she'd been waiting for, the evidence she needed to take down the cartel. Heart pounding, she pulled her woolen cap down tight to conceal her blonde hair and dropped to crawl through the bushes. This building was used for storing barrels of wine and was an unusual place for the pickup of a consignment. Carlos Winery sold its wine in bottles and the secrecy surrounding the blending of the fine wines made the idea of selling barrels of the precious aged nectar ludicrous. As the doors slid open, she pressed her binoculars to her eyes and blinked in astonishment as, beyond the rows of stacked casks, a wall slid back to display a brightly lit room filled with people wearing hazmat suits and working on stainless steel benches.

Her attention went to the trays of a glistening ice-like substance, recognizing it at once as crystal meth. Workers moved plastic bags filled with the drug from the table to a line of barrels. Once packed, they sealed the barrels and marked them on the side using a special stencil. As they filled each barrel, it was loaded onto a truck. It was the proof she needed. She raised her camera and zoomed in. The high-resolution images could be enlarged without distortion but getting closer to take pictures of the main players would seal the deal. At this angle, all the men in suits had their backs to her and she dashed across open ground to the next building. Panting more with fear than overexertion, she hit the ground and rolled onto her belly. The camera clicked, taking the shots she needed, but if anyone looked her way, they'd discover her.

As one truck left, another rumbled up and backed slowly to the entrance. The headlights swept the area, including her hiding place. She flattened against the damp earth, too frightened to breathe. Being married to Michael Carlos meant nothing to her safety. He and his father, Viktor, were ruthless and unforgiving. If they found her spying on them, there'd be no mercy. The lights moved again as the truck backed closer to the entrance and shadows bathed her.

Voices and desperate pleas came from inside the building, the sound coming to her as crystal clear as if from an amphitheater. Accusations of theft of the product and threats of the consequences. There would be no mercy for this man. She lifted her head as two men dragged a beaten man from inside and tossed him at the feet of her husband. Trembling in horror, she held the camera to her eye and kept taking photographs. The way Michael spoke to the man and then spat on him terrified her. It was the voice of a psychopath, unfeeling and brutal. Panic gripped her as Michael calmly pulled out a pistol, twirled a suppressor onto the muzzle, and calmly shot the man in the head. Not one person reacted, as if blowing out a man's brains was common practice. After a short discussion, his henchmen dragged the body across the lawn and tossed it into a pit right outside the bottling plant. The cement trucks were due at six the next morning to fill the foundation of a pergola to be erected for visitors to enjoy on wine-tasting tours. Teeth chattering with shock, Avril froze as one of the workers, hosed down the area, washing away all traces of blood. Men seemingly oblivious to the murder right in front of them worked swiftly using forklifts to lift barrels tied to pallets onto the truck. The guards and Michael constantly scanned the grounds as if they knew she lay watching them.

As ants crawled over her, Avril remained motionless until the truck moved again, laden with casks, hiding millions of dollars' worth of drugs on their way to the street hustlers. She rolled over and stared at the stars, trying to process the enormity of what she'd seen. It had been her mission to uncover Carlos's operation, and she'd hit the jackpot. It had been so well hidden for so many years and, having the winery, the business offices, and residences encapsulated inside a restricted estate, it was as secure as Fort Knox. The fenced vineyards extended over the surrounding picturesque hills, and the grapevines had workers tending them year-round with loving care, but the mysteries surrounding vintner Viktor Carlos's secret blend, including the buildings containing the massive stainless steel vats, the specially treated oak barrels, and the extensive cellars holding thousands of bottles of wine, were kept as secure as gold.

During her time at the winery, she'd watched and listened for any hint of the drug business, but no one ever mentioned a word. Ready to give up and be evacuated from the mission, she'd overheard Michael mention the word *shift* in relation to the workers. She'd not been aware of any shift workers and made sure to watch the staff coming and going a little closer.

Where the extent of the workforce had been working hadn't been an issue until now. In her job arranging winery tours and dinners for the guests, she had access to the computer system. In the files, she'd found less than half the workforce she'd seen arriving each morning on the books and decided to follow up. She swallowed hard. Luck must have been on her side to stumble over a meth lab on the way to Michael's office.

The end to the mission loomed ahead of her like a guiding light. It had been tough, fighting through the suffering of Michael's constant abuse, all the time acting the doting wife. He treated her like property and enjoyed making her suffer. Because of her implied disposability, her initial plan to sneak out tonight to search his office had placed her in a perilous situation. Even more so now, after witnessing his ruthlessness first-hand. If discovered, she'd disappear and become another one of the winery's garden features. She gave herself a mental shake. *Stick to the plan and go search the office.*

The increase in security and staff now made sense, but who else was involved? She'd figured searching Michael's office for evidence was crucial and she might only have the one chance. She'd been lying fully clothed in bed when she'd heard him drive away and had snuck out of the house. If he'd taken his sedan, he wouldn't be going to the office. That was for sure. The building was within walking distance, and she'd planned to dash there and back long before he returned. Earlier in the day, she'd gone by his office and dropped her engagement ring behind the filing cabinet as an excuse to be there, if he returned and discovered her in his office, late at night. She'd rehearsed her story and would tell him she'd lost her ring, couldn't sleep with the worry, and decided to retrace her steps before the cleaners arrived in the early hours.

Her plans had changed on the way to the office building when she'd spotted Michael's sedan bathed in the lights spilling from the cask storage area, and she changed course to investigate. The discovery of a meth lab had made the need to find the extent of the players in the syndicate urgent—she had to search his office and time was running out fast. Biting her bottom lip, she gathered her courage. It was lucky that Michael wasn't the brightest peg on the rack and had a habit of writing important times and dates in a desk diary. He was old school, leaving his secretary to file manifests and other important information for the company on the computer, but Avril doubted the distribution of crystal meth was in her job description. Knowing Michael's bad memory, he'd likely written a note for himself. All she had to do was discover the main players involved in the drug shipments, and with these names added to the images she'd just taken, she'd have enough evidence to take down the cartel.

Keeping to the shadows, she slipped through the bushes and made her way to the office building. She'd learned the code to the door, so getting inside wouldn't be a problem. Lights blazed in the foyer as usual, but also spilled from the windows of both Michael's and his father Viktor's offices, which was unusual for a Sunday. Avril straightened and pushed at the glass door and, finding it open, walked inside and headed for the bathroom. She thrust her hat and gloves deep inside her pockets and then checked her appearance. After brushing the leaves from her clothes, and then washing her hands and face, she raked her fingers through her hair. Heart hammering, she lifted her chin and headed for Michael's office. Acting as if she owned the place and had the right to be there was part of the deception, no matter how her stomach cramped with fear. As she reached the office, she called out his name, like an innocent wife seeking her husband would do, and peered inside the office just in case her father-in-law was lurking close by. The scent of his cologne greeted her as if he'd just left the room and gave her the feeling that he was watching her as she stepped inside. She had a few minutes to get in and out without being seen and pushed down the rising panic. After closing the door behind her, she scanned Michael's desk and found nothing of interest, but her attention fixed on a bunch of keys hanging from the lock in the desk drawer.

Listening for any sound, she tugged at the handle and the drawer slid open. She couldn't believe her luck. Right on the top of a stack of papers was his diary. Lifting out the red leather-bound volume, she flipped through the pages until she found today's date and scanned the page. The date and time references coincided with the coming and going of trucks late at night. It gave amounts listed in hundreds and the number of barrels required. The only problem was the receiver of the goods was in code or perhaps initials, but the destination was clear. It couldn't be wine; The three women working in the office handled the wine orders and it wasn't Michael but his father, Viktor Carlos, who negotiated the terms to supply restaurants, hotels, and overseas orders, so this information must refer to the movement of drugs. From what she could see, this was Michael's field of expertise.

She flipped back and forth and, using the camera from the heel of her boot, took pictures of anything incriminating. A slight click like a door opening along the hallway was as loud as a gunshot in the silence. Heart thundering, she pushed the book back inside the drawer as the distinctive sound of footsteps came toward her. She couldn't allow anyone to find her spying on her husband and dropped to the floor. She thrust the camera back inside the heel of her boot and with her heart in her mouth, turned to stare at the door. Perspiration trickled between her shoulder blades as the doorknob turned slowly and the door brushed across the thick wool carpet. Unable to breathe with fear, she rolled to all fours and bent her face to the floor to peer under the office furniture. She could see her ring, a gold and diamond circle between the wall and the filing cabinet. The door opened wide and feigning surprise she turned her head to greet the man standing in the doorway looking at her with a deep frown. She pressed one hand to her chest and smiled. "Oh, thank goodness it's you, Viktor. I need your help."

"Do you know what time it is?" Viktor Carlos peered suspiciously around the room. "What are you doing snooping around Michael's office at this time of night?"

Terrified but acting nonchalant, Avril sat up and forced her lips into a smile. "Oh, I wasn't sneaking around, Viktor. I called out when I arrived. With all the lights blazing, I had hoped someone was here. It's a frightening place at night." She gave an exasperated sigh. "I just had to come over tonight. I haven't told Michael, but I lost my engagement ring today. It's loose and must have slipped off my finger. I've been searching all day for it and couldn't recall where I'd last seen it. I was fast asleep and woke up. Just like that, I remembered the last placed I'd been before I noticed it was missing."

"And where was that?" Viktor's eyes moved over her. "Crawling on the floor in my son's office?"

Trying to look confused, Avril waved a hand toward the filing cabinet. "Of course not. I came over earlier to talk to Michael about the auction dinner and noticed the plant on the filing cabinet needed watering. I remember spilling water over my hand. I guess the ring slipped off when I was returning the plant. I knew Michael was working late, so I dashed over to see if my ring was on the floor before the cleaners arrive." She indicated to the filing cabinet. "I found it! It's behind here. Can you move the filing cabinet for me?"

"No." Viktor narrowed his gaze at her. He went to the desk, retrieved the keys, and opened the filing cabinet. "Slide out the bottom drawer and you should be able to reach it."

She followed his instructions and retrieved the ring, acting as girly as possible. They seemed to like her to be weak and dependent. With Michael's violent outbursts, it had taken every bit of her self-control to take his punishment and not fight back.

If only he knew how easily she could hurt him and how many times she'd wanted to defend herself.

Standing, she slipped the ring back on her finger. "Now I can get a good night's sleep. Thanks for your help." She squeezed his arm and noticed his mood change at once. He'd believed her.

"This will be our little secret. Michael wouldn't like to know you've been running around after dark alone." Viktor gave her a nod. "Hurry back to bed." He dismissed her like a child.

TWO

Avril headed back to the house, her mind spinning. Everything she'd worked toward had come to fruition in one night, but getting the information to her contact in town wasn't so easy. Her next scheduled meeting was four days away. Not a face-to-face meeting, but by means of a note written in code on a ten-dollar bill or a fake coin dropped into a busker's hat. She had to use every bit of cunning she possessed because Michael Carlos refused to allow her to go anywhere alone. She'd become his very well-cared-for prisoner.

It had taken Avril almost two long years to infiltrate the inner sanctum of the cartel run by underworld kingpin Viktor Carlos. The DEA had suspected for some time that the Carlos family business was involved in the trafficking of billions of dollars' worth of drugs, but assumed they were just the tip of the iceberg. Walls of secrecy surrounded the family and the DEA had not one shred of evidence against them. On face value, they appeared to be running a legitimate and very successful winery. Her assignment was to go in deep and get the proof they needed and the names of everyone involved. After living on the edge and lowering herself into the depths of depravity by marrying

Viktor's son, Michael, it was finally paying off. As Avril Carlos, she enjoyed the status of a trophy wife and lived on the family estate, free to move around. She now had evidence that the vast empire known as Carlos Vineyards acted as the cover for the manufacture and distribution of crystal meth, known on the streets as "ice."

The sound of a vehicle rumbled to a stop outside the front of the house. Panic gripped Avril and, dragging off her coat and pushing her hat into the pocket, she slipped inside the back door. In the mudroom, she hung up her coat and removed her sweatpants and tossed them into the washer. Stowing her boots in their usual place, she pushed on the slippers she'd left by the door and smoothed down her nightgown. The grandfather clock in the hallway finished chiming, telling her it was two in the morning when light footsteps came from behind her. She didn't turn around but casually reached to take a glass from the kitchen shelf and fill it at the sink. Sipping the cool water, she stood in the darkness, peering out the window into the moonlit garden.

"What are you doing out of bed?" Michael's hands rested lightly on her shoulders but they might as well have been a noose around her neck.

Trying not to flinch under his touch, she continued to stare out of the window. "I couldn't sleep. I like looking at the garden in the moonlight. I like to walk in the moonlight too—you know that. We used to do it together at one time." She placed the glass on the bench. "You're home late. You work too hard."

"I had business to attend to with my father. It's nothing for you to worry about." He turned her around to face him. "In the morning, I'll have a surprise for you. It will stop you moping around. Go up to bed."

He'd dismissed her and she hurried away like the obedient wife he expected her to be. She would slip back down the moment he'd gone to sleep and retrieve the micro card from her camera. Michael had lost interest in her six months after their marriage because she hadn't become pregnant. An impossibility due to a contraceptive implant. He now used her to welcome wealthy buyers, host parties, and be a spokesperson for the winery. She had her own room and it was a relief to be away from him—he made her skin crawl. Avril hoped the sham marriage and prostituting herself with Michael to gain the cartel's trust had been worth it, not only to stop the distribution of illegal drugs but to see him in jail for the rest of his life. The fact he used the servants for his pleasure was actually a relief and to them it seemed being his mistress was a status symbol. Most had looked at her as if they felt sorry for her or became so arrogant at gaining her husband's favors that she'd complained. Michael had just shrugged and she assumed he'd sent them to work somewhere else on the massive estate because she never saw them again. Although the moment one left, a new beautiful woman would be serving their meals or cleaning the house, but Michael never said a word in protest. Apart from the hiring and firing of staff, she controlled the day-to-day running of the house. It was her domain and was the only part of her life he didn't control.

Before daylight, she snuck down to the mudroom to retrieve the camera and binoculars. She returned the binoculars to her nightstand; they'd been a purchase she'd made on the pretense of birdwatching. After removing the microcard from the camera and hiding it in the back of her watch, she flushed the tiny device down the toilet. Nerves on a knife edge, she paced her bedroom. The information she had was gold, but would Viktor tell Michael he'd found her in the office? If Michael gave her another beating, he'd keep her home until the bruises faded. She chewed on her bottom lip. Anything might happen before her next visit to town and she had to pass on the information—now. Avril usually contacted Steve Breuer on a regular shopping trip. She'd walk by him and drop a few bills into his hat as he sat in the park playing his guitar disguised as a homeless man. This time she'd add a fake one-dollar coin containing the microcard. DEA Agent Steve Breuer wasn't only her contact with the outside world. He was a close friend and having him around even at a distance was comforting. But no plan was foolproof, and if everything went to hell, her failsafe was Nurse Jenkins. The woman worked at the local doctor's office, where Avril could go or call in an emergency.

She'd met Steve at work and they'd started dating. The six months they'd had together had been like a wonderful dream and they'd made plans for the future. When the assignment came through, Steve hadn't stood in her way but encouraged her to do the job she'd been trained to do. Not wanting her to be undercover alone, he'd volunteered to live on the streets and act as her contact. He was strong, reliable, and she loved him. They had a bond of trust between them, and if she got into trouble, he'd be there watching her back. Meeting him was fast becoming a problem and she worried her bodyguard might notice her interest in the busker. After changing her routine, she'd sit in the park and drink coffee, making sure Steve had seen her. Avoiding him was the only way to keep him safe but now she had no choice. This time would be the last and the entire mission depended on passing on the information. She smiled, imagining the celebration they'd have when they walked back into the DEA office. She'd cracked the case, and her and Steve's nightmare assignments would be over. She would have enough evidence to put the Carlos cartel behind bars, and life would hopefully return to some type of normal.

THREE

The following morning, Michael ushered a young girl into her room. The Asian girl was small, perhaps eight years old or so, and kept her eyes fixed on the floor. She was wearing an ill-fitting shift and sandals. From what Avril could see, she looked miserable. "Who is this?"

"This is Mandy." Michael stroked the girl's hair as if she were a puppy. "Well, that's as close as I can get to pronouncing her name. Her family was from Vietnam and she's staying with us for a time." He grinned. "This is your surprise. Isn't she adorable? She'll work very hard to please you."

Avril stared at him in disbelief. Bringing a child into a drug cartel was fraught with danger. She had to object. "Really? I don't really have the time to babysit a kid. She should be in school. Does she even speak English?"

"No, and we'll work all that out. In the meantime, find her something to do." He let out an exasperated sigh. "If you get bored with her, send her to her room. I've put her in the nursery and I'll have toys and books sent up. It's all arranged."

Unconvinced, Avril pushed the breakfast tray a servant had

brought her to one side and lifted her chin. "You're in the wine business. Since when did you give a damn about orphans?"

"Well, you couldn't give me a child, could you?" Michael's eyes flashed. "Mandy stays until I decide otherwise. I'll send a car around for you at ten. Take her into town and buy her some clothes, ribbons for her hair, those socks with lace on the top. All the pretty things. See if you can teach her some English. If you can settle her into being here, it will help other girls like her to understand our ways. She'll be able to explain to them in her own language that they've come to a better place. I know wealthy families willing to take the pretty ones."

Alarmed, Avril leaped out of bed. "What on earth are you saying, Michael? Where did she come from? If she's a runaway, you need to call the cops. You can't just keep her or give her to someone else. That's crazy. She's a person not a damn dog."

"That's none of your concern. Trust me, she's not a runaway. She's an illegal, okay? One of the workers came to me asking for my help. He told me he'd found kids like her separated from their families and left to fend for themselves." He lifted his arms and dropped them. "What did you expect me to do, Avril? Turn her away? We have a big empty house and I'm prepared to adopt her if you agree. I want to help as many of them as possible. You should be encouraging me to help her, instead of looking at me like that."

Unconvinced, Avril shook her head. "Is what you're proposing even legal? Your father will be as mad as hell if you get into trouble with the law. Does he know about this?"

"Yeah, and he agrees with me about these girls—and yes, the legalities are already sorted." He took her hand and stroked it as if it made everything right. "I spoke to Judge Arnold and he assures me he can make all the adoptions legal. He'll handle everything. We'll have the child we always wanted and maybe more, later on, if she works out."

Oh, he was good. He could convince a snake to skin itself.

She sighed, taking in the forlorn figure still staring at the floor. The DEA agent in her wanted to scream a protest from the rooftops. Judge Arnold would be spending a lifetime in jail for running an illegal adoptions racket when she'd finished with him, but right now, she had to go along with whatever Michael wanted. She had no choice as anything else would jeopardize her mission and likely cost her her life. At least she could offer the girl her protection and get her back to her family when she'd brought the cartel to justice. "Okay. If you're sure it's legal. I'll help." She gently pulled her hand from his and forced her lips into a smile.

"I knew you'd see it my way, if I explained things." He tossed a credit card on the bed. "Go shopping but don't take all day. There are tours of the vineyard to plan. I've a ton of important visitors due this month, so buy what you need for yourself to impress them. Now, I have a business to run. We'll talk again later." He headed out the door.

Avril picked up the phone and spoke to the housekeeper. "Do you have any old clothes, suitable for an eight-year-old?" She listened for a moment. "Just one set. I'll have them back to you within the day." She turned and looked at the girl. "Are you a companion or a spy?" She pointed to a chair and urged her to sit. "Wait here. I need to take a shower."

Under the waterflow, Avril's mind was moving at warp speed. If she went into town today, Michael would never expect her to go back in a few days. If she didn't meet her contact, the agency would go on alert and the two years of her life she'd given trying to bring down the cartel would be ruined. She had to think fast. Getting the proof about the drug manufacturing to her contact was a priority. Now Michael had thrown her a curveball and given her a little girl to care for. She'd need to find out more about Mandy, and fast, but right now, her priority was an excuse to be in town in four days.

FOUR

As usual, Michael supplied a limousine and a bodyguard for any trip Avril made into town. The security was suffocating and only by insisting she required a modicum of privacy did Michael allow her to enter the stores alone to purchase clothes or visit the doctor. She stepped out into the Californian sunshine, adjusted her hat and, taking Mandy's hand, led her into one of the high-end children's fashion stores. She took a seat in the vanilla-scented store and allowed the saleslady to outfit Mandy with a selection of fifteen outfits, sleepwear, underwear, and socks. After dressing Mandy in a new outfit, Avril headed for the shoe store and selected suitable pairs for Mandy and herself. The little girl seemed to be very compliant and didn't make a sound, just followed her in silence. Avril wondered if she could actually speak. The shopping was the only part of being undercover she enjoyed. It seemed Michael had unlimited funds and never questioned the amount she spent, so she splurged on everything from designer clothes to cosmetics. The parcels wrapped, she waved the bodyguard inside the store to collect them. She never carried anything more than her purse, containing a phone, which Michael checked regularly when he believed her to be asleep; a credit card he issued only when required; and the generous cash allowance he gave her after she insisted she needed a few bills to pay for coffee and anything else that took her fancy.

As she waited for Mandy to try on suitable shoes, she glanced out of the window at the Vietnamese restaurant across the road. Seeing it set off a lightbulb in her head. She looked at the nameless bodyguard. Michael had never allowed any kind of intimacy between them, not even giving her his name. "I'm going to the restaurant over there. Wait here." She took Mandy by the hand and waited at the curb of the busy road for a break in the traffic.

"Okay." The man leaned in the window of the limo to speak to the driver, but ignored her orders and followed her across the road to wait outside for her.

Inside the restaurant, Avril inhaled the rich spicy aromas and looked all around before heading to the take-out counter. The woman looked from her to Mandy and then raised both eyebrows. She smiled at her. "I wonder if you could help me?"

"You want to buy food? The menu is here on the counter." The woman pointed to the folded plastic sheet. "The specials are on the blackboard."

"I would like to buy some of your time and perhaps a meal for Mandy." Avril indicated to the girl.

"Why do you want to pay for my time?" The woman gave her a puzzled look. "Do I look like a hooker?"

"Oh no, of course not. Allow me to explain." Avril pulled a hundred-dollar bill from her purse and placed it on the counter. "I'm fostering Mandy until we can locate her parents. She doesn't speak English. I need someone to ask her some questions and perhaps help her learn a few words of English so I can communicate better with her." She met the woman's gaze. "If you can help me, the money is yours and, of course, I'll pay for the meal separately. I want Mandy to feel at home while she is with us."

"Why didn't they place her with a Vietnamese family?" The woman narrowed her gaze. "We have a different culture than you, different ways. She should be with her own people."

Avril nodded. "I agree, but for now, she's in my care. Will you help me or not?"

"Yes." The woman turned and called out something. Moments later, a younger woman came from the back. "I have ordered some food for her. Come inside and we'll talk." She led them to a quiet booth at the back of the restaurant near the kitchen.

The woman smiled at Mandy and the girl responded, but she seemed to be sluggish and kept blinking her eyes as if trying to stay awake. After a few minutes the woman stared at Avril unblinking. "What is it? Did you find out anything?"

"Yes, I did."

The food came out and the little girl ate slowly, ignoring everyone and just staring at her plate. Avril cleared her throat. "What did she say?"

"Her name is Ly Mai. Her first name is Mai. She and her sister and parents were on a ship that stunk of fish. Her father vanished. She said he went with some men and never returned. Same with her mother. Her sister was with her when they left the boat, but the men separated them. They gave her food and drink and she fell asleep and woke up in your house. A man called her Mandy and gave her another drink that made her head feel funny. Then she met you. She likes you." The woman studied her face. "Has she been drugged?"

The idea had crossed Avril's mind. She smiled. It seemed she had become a convincing liar and could pull one out of the air without a second thought. "I believe the doctor who checked her out gave her a sedative. She was hysterical when she arrived. Can you tell her she can trust me and that I'll care for her? Tell her I'm trying to find her family."

The woman spoke rapidly and the girl nodded before saying something. Avril looked at the woman. "What did she say?"

"She called you friend. *Ban be*."

The pronunciation sounded like "bat bey" and Avril smiled and touched her chest. "Avril... *Ban be*."

The little girl repeated the word but not her name. Avril smiled at her and then turned to the woman. "Do you know of anyone who could give her English lessons? We need to be able to communicate with her. I'll pay whatever it costs. I live at Carlos Winery."

"Oh, I know who you are, Mrs. Carlos." The woman nodded, but her expression wasn't at all friendly. "If you'll leave me your details. I'll see what I can do."

Avril nodded. "Thank you."

As Mai finished her meal, Avril wrote down her phone number and handed it to the woman. "I'm happy to pay cash for the lessons. Money isn't a problem. I just want to make her happy."

She stood and, taking Mai's hand, led her from the restaurant. As she stepped onto the sidewalk, she ran slap bang into her dentist. They chatted for a few moments about her tardiness at getting her checkups and Avril smiled. It was the first time in her life she'd welcomed a visit to the dentist. "How about Thursday? I'm coming into town to do some shopping."

"Wait just a second." The dentist called his office and smiled at her. "I can fit you in at eleven, how does that sound?" He pulled a business card out of his pocket and scribbled the time and date of the appointment and handed it to her. "See you then."

Avril stared at the card. The bodyguard had heard every word and would report back to Michael. She smiled to herself as she pushed the card into her purse. Now she had a legitimate reason to be in town on Thursday.

FIVE

Over the next few days, Avril spent much of her daylight hours with Mai. A delightful child who wanted to please her by learning English, she soon had a few words in her vocabulary. It had surprised her how attached she'd become to the little girl and the plans to take her with her when she escaped her own personal hell had been uppermost in her mind. In the middle of the night, she snuck out again to confirm the movement of the drugs. It seemed the shipments went out Sunday through Wednesday nights and these times coincided with the previous times she'd heard Michael leave and return to the house.

During the day, she took Mai with her everywhere, organizing wine tours and a new regular special event that Michael and Viktor had spoken to her about with enthusiasm. The guest list for the special event was a closely guarded secret. Good food and their best wine would be served before Viktor held a secret auction of their finest bottles of wine. She'd made the arrangements, and only their trusted staff members would be serving their guests. Avril stood in front of Viktor's polished oak desk, her knees slightly shaking. "Why all the secrecy? Surely if one of your bottles of wine goes for an incredible price, you'd want people to know about it."

"Our clients prefer confidentiality." Viktor's cold eyes settled on her face. "You'll make all the arrangements and greet our guests, but the auction is for the bidders only." His gaze moved to Mai, seated in a huge leather chair. "Enough about the auction. Has Michael explained about the orphans? I've received information about others living alone on the streets and have asked my people to round them up." He steepled his fingers and smiled. "Michael convinced me it's the humanitarian thing to do. Don't you agree?" He indicated to Mai. "Look at her. In just three days she's a different child. Like you and Michael, there are many childless couples out there who'd offer a similar girl a home. Wealthy couples would dote on them. We just need Mai to convince these kids to go with them willingly. No one will be happy with a belligerent child." He sighed. "Michael tells me she is very compliant. We need them all to be the same. It's fortunate in their culture they respect their elders. It will make things easier."

Avril frowned. Since when had Viktor Carlos thought about anyone but himself? She forced down the rush of uncertainty. If anything was amiss, she'd be able to trace the children through Judge Arnold and put things right. For now, she had to focus on obliterating the cartel. Forcing her lips into a smile, she lifted her chin. "I'll help in any way I can. I'm already attached to Mai, and Michael is thinking of adoption."

"Is he now?" Viktor gave a belly laugh. "Did he ever tell you about the puppy his mother gave him for his birthday? God rest her soul."

Not wanting to know, Avril shook her head. "I'll ask him one day, but right now I must get back to work. The auction will take a lot of organizing." She gathered her things. "Are we done here?"

"Yeah, we're done." Viktor smiled at her. "Don't get too

attached to her. I'm told there are plenty to choose from and I'm sure Michael has yet to make his choice."

What a strange turn of phrase? Avril hurried for the door, grabbing Mai's hand on the way.

* * *

Thursday arrived and Avril had everything for the auction the following Friday night arranged in warp speed so she could leave the estate and supposedly visit the dentist. Exhilaration thrummed through her at the chance to finally get the evidence on the cartel to the DEA. She carried a tiny, yet powerful camera, microcards, and hollow coins. These she kept stashed in the heels of a pair of shoes. She'd added the secret code to the ten-dollar bill and would drop it along with the fake dollar coin containing the microcard into undercover DEA Agent Steve Breuer's busker's hat. He would communicate her message to her handler and then get the hell out of Dodge. His work would be over.

It had taken her a long time to get inside Viktor Carlos's closely guarded circle. Impossible, in fact, and the only chance she'd had was through his son. It hadn't been easy getting close to Michael Carlos, but fortunately he liked blondes. She'd made herself available by always being at clubs he frequented, and it hadn't taken anytime at all for him to notice her. From then on, being the perfect girlfriend and then his wife, she'd become seemingly oblivious to the family's secret dealings, armed guards, and electric fences. The hazardous move had paid out in silver dollars. Michael trusted her, but he had a jealous streak a mile wide. He didn't want her, but nobody else could have her either. He limited himself to checking her phone and sometimes her shopping bags but was apparently content she had no other male interests. Although, he expected her to be on show twenty-four/seven as a frontperson for the business, and had her face plastered all over the brochures for the winery tours.

As usual, she went to Michael's office to inform him she'd be leaving. His secretary was sitting at her desk filing her nails and flicked her a glance as she rested a hand on the door. Hearing conversation, she looked at the secretary. "Is he alone?"

"Yeah." She didn't as much as look up at her. "He's on the phone."

Avril opened the door and led Mai inside. The conversation was about shipments, or rather ships. The trucks had been waiting for a ship to dock and some supplies had been held up in customs. She bit her bottom lip. Orders had been given that, during the sting operation, customs were to allow Carlos's cargo free passage, without any holdups. She cleared her throat. "What's happening?"

"It's customs." Michael rolled his eyes. "I ordered supplies and they're playing hardball. Seems the crew we usually have on the docks has been relocated."

It would be dangerous to contact anyone in her team but the incoming shipment was likely to be the bulk chemicals the factory required to make "ice." Without these, the production would cease and she'd have no proof to offer for a raid. She swallowed the bile creeping up the back of her throat and smiled. "I have a few contacts I could try. Watch Mai for me. I'll go to my office and see if I can find the number."

Heart thumping, she dashed to her office, made a call on her cellphone to the harbormaster, asked him a stupid question, disconnected, and then called a memorized number. It took her a few seconds to identify herself, state the problem, disconnect, and then delete all evidence of her call from her phone. If Michael checked up on her, he'd only find the first number called. She stood and walked slowly back to his office. On opening the door, she was surprised to see Mai sitting on his lap. The young girl looked a little confused. Avril held out her hand.

"It's all fixed. I have to go. My dentist appointment is at eleven and I'd like to get a few things done beforehand. Come on, Mai."

"Why don't you leave her with me today?" He stroked Mai's hair. "We can get to know each other better."

Not liking the amusement in his eyes, Avril shook her head. "Not today." She took the little girl's hand and pulled him from him. "We have girl things to do. I'll need my card. I've seen a diamond necklace I want to buy for the dinner. You want me to look the part, don't you?"

"I spoil you." Michael cupped her face and squeezed. "It's just as well you get more beautiful by the day because I'm losing my patience. No one comes close to you, Avril. I miss the fight in your eyes. It's time you came back to my bed." He pulled the card from his wallet and handed it to her. "This card may not have a limit, but I do." He gave her a long look. "Hurry back."

She looked at the card with the name Avril Carlos and smiled. "Thank you. We'll talk later."

The card had her name, but she didn't own it. Like her, it was one of his possessions. She headed back to the house and went to speak to the housekeeper. "Arrange to have Mai's bed moved into my room. She's having bad dreams."

Without waiting for a reply, she headed for the front door. The men's sudden interest in young girls had her mind working overtime. Something wasn't right and she had to get to the bottom of it before the agency rolled into action and intercepted the trucks on Sunday night. The special occasion for the rich and famous was a clue she hadn't missed and her instinct told her the answers she needed centered around it. The tension in the situation was reaching critical mass. She chewed on her fingers. The auction had to be a front for something else or why all the secrecy? She had to find a way of sneaking inside to find out. If she discovered another arm to the crime empire of Viktor Carlos or not, she'd take the girl and make a run for it. She'd add a message to the note for her contact to tell the bureau that she wanted out on Friday night, and to evacuate her before daybreak.

She hurried to the limousine awaiting her. Inside, as the car rolled through the picturesque rolling vineyards, she pulled out the ten-dollar bill she intended to drop into the busker's hat. She was well hidden behind the tinted glass partition between her and the driver and bodyguard. She added an addition to her coded information: *Important development. Emergency evac. Midnight Friday from town.*

SIX

It was a little after ten when Avril arrived in town. She instructed the driver to pull up some ways from the dentist's office and she strolled through the streets window-shopping. She could hear the soft notes of the guitar played by Steve Breuer coming from the park. It was his usual place, sitting on the edge of the fountain, a ratty hat before him on the sidewalk. He looked unkempt, his dark hair shaggy and hanging way past his collar. He played the guitar as if it were an extension of his hands, the music mesmerizing. Steve, in his way, had kept her going. Just knowing someone knew her true identity and what she was doing after so long out in the world alone made her strong. Being so deep undercover, she understood now how some agents could be turned, but not her. Her determination to get a job done was how she'd landed this mission—well, that and the fact after losing her family she'd been alone. With no family to threaten, the only thing Viktor Carlos could take from her was her life. Being a natural blonde had tipped the agency in her favor, but she realized now she'd been a little too young and lacked experience. Avril didn't have the street smarts she needed and, in truth, she'd only survived by using her gut instinct.

She led Mai through the fragrant rose gardens, set in neatly bordered circles amid a luscious green lawn, and headed for the fountain. She stopped to listen to Steve and passed the bills and coins to Mai to drop into her contact's hat. The little girl seemed to understand the concept of busking and smiled and clapped her hands as the song came to an end.

"Why, thank you, little one." Steve smiled broadly. His eyes never left Mai. "Maybe when I get off the streets, I'll take you and your mom out for ice cream." He looked up at her. "What do you say, Mom?'

Astonished, Avril gaped at him. "Ah, no thank you."

"One day." Steve chuckled and plucked his guitar.

Panic gripped Avril. Her bodyguard was close enough to have heard him. Without doubt, he would pass on the information to Michael the second she arrived home. She moved away not saying a word and, heart thundering, kept on walking. She could hear the bodyguard's steady footsteps behind her—always watching, always there—like an ugly dangerous shadow.

Eyes staring straight ahead, and holding Mai's hand, she made it into the dentist's building without a comment from the bodyguard. Things could get nasty and she needed a plan B. She pulled out the credit card and turned it in her hands. All the agents she'd known had some type of an exit strategy or a get-out-of-jail-free card, and she'd made plans ahead of time, but executing them could be the last nail in her coffin. She glanced down at Mai. "I'm out of options."

Once inside the dentist's office, she apologized for having a headache and made another appointment to appease them. After taking the back stairs, she slipped out the side exit and into the bank on the next block. She asked to see the manager and, as the Carlos Winery was one of the bank's biggest customers, a woman ushered her into his office. She noticed his glance shifting to Mai and she smiled. "I'm caring for her." She cleared her throat. "I need to make a substantial transfer and require the balance of my account."

"It's a joint account, as you know." The manager smiled. "One of many you have at our branch." He gave her a figure that made her jaw drop.

Avril grabbed a pen and wrote down the number of an offshore bank account she'd set up with a small amount of cash to use if everything went to hell. Right now, she needed more than her handler's assurance he'd pull her to safety the moment she gave the word. Viktor Carlos had fingers in every pie and she would never be safe if he discovered what she'd done. "Yes, that sounds about right." She pushed the account number across the table toward him and stared him straight in the eye. *Act like you own this bank, Avril.* "Transfer ten million into that account for me please."

"That's a large amount. Should I clear it with Mr. Carlos first?"

Avril laughed. "Oh, really, and spoil my surprise?" She patted his hand. "It's a gift. A parcel of land in the Napa Valley he's wanted for years. This will seal the deal."

"But this is an offshore account." The manager's head beaded in sweat. "Once it's transferred its untraceable. If you change your mind, it's lost forever."

Grinning like a baboon, Avril met his gaze. "Oh, I know it's a little unconventional but you make transfers like this for Michael all the time, don't you? I *am* his wife, in case it slipped your mind?" She stopped grinning. "It's my money. Make the transfer or I'll speak to my father-in-law. One complaint from me and he'll have his account moved to another, more compliant bank." She stood and moved around the desk. "I'll watch the transfer if you don't mind."

When the money went through, she leaned on the desk and eyeballed him. "This deal was made by my father-in-law. It's a joint gift from the both of us. Not a word to Michael. If you spoil our surprise, Viktor will be down to speak to you personally." She straightened, collected her card, and held a hand out to Mai. "Come on now, it's time to go home."

SEVEN

Late that afternoon, Avril sat with Mai in the nursery as her English teacher went over a few phrases. The little girl was mastering the language quickly and practiced all the time. She heard voices outside the door. Michael was in the house, which was unusual during the day, especially when they had the auction later. She assumed he'd be checking over the plans she'd made. He had always stood over her, watching as if waiting to pounce if she made a mistake, but she'd only just left the hall and everything was moving along smoothly. The food was arranged, the staff had already organized the hall, and she'd be there to greet the guests at seven. The auction of vintage wines was Michael and his father's domain, as was the guest list. So why the raised voices?

She smiled at Mai and slipped out into the hallway. The next second, Michael grabbed her arm and spun her to face him. Anger radiated from him, but his slap came as a surprise, and as the metallic taste of blood filled her mouth, she stared at him in shock.

"Whore." Michael's eyes blazed with hatred as he struck

her again. "You'd drag my name into the gutter by hanging all over a panhandler?"

Before she could speak, he dragged her through the house and across the lawn to an outbuilding. She dug in her heels. "Stop it, you're hurting me."

"Walk or I'll drag you by your hair." Michael's eyes glittered with menace. "It's time for you to understand what happens when you don't obey me."

Breathing hard, she tried to break his steel-like grip crushing her arm. "What are you talking about? I've done everything you've asked."

"Your lover doesn't look so good now, does he?" Michael shoved her into the building.

Avril blinked in the dim light and gaped in horror as the stink of blood and pee enclosed her. Steve Breuer, bloody and battered, hung from his arms in the middle of the room. A crimson-smeared baseball bat lay at his feet. Had Michael found her message and the coin with the damning evidence inside or had Steve managed to send it in time? Was she about to face the same lesson? Pushed closer, she stared at Steve in the gloom, her throat so tight with fear she dared not take a breath. He wasn't moving, and she'd seen eyes fixed in death before. The pain of loss swept over her and her knees threatened to buckle. Digging her fingernails deep into her palms, she fought to keep control of her emotions. Her heart raced and she wanted to vomit. Michael had killed him, but Steve hadn't said a word or she'd be dead too. Her survival instinct kicked in and, biting back the need to scream and attack the monster beside her, she gritted her teeth. Steeling herself with every ounce of courage she had, she composed her features and turned to Michael. "Who the hell is that?"

"Your music man. The man you hang all over every damn time you go to town. Don't you recognize him?" He sneered at her. "Don't you think the bodyguards report your every movement to me? I own you. You're my property. I can do what I want with you." He raised his hand to strike her again.

Avril sidestepped and lifted her chin, glad for the calm her training had instilled in her. "Go ahead and I'll look real pretty when I greet your guests. Will it make you look like a big man, showing them how you treat your wife?" She waved a hand at the beaten man. There was nothing she could do for him now, but she must survive long enough to bring this animal to justice. "Do you honestly believe I'd stoop so low, Michael? A busker—really? I liked his music and felt sorry for him is all. I dropped a few dollars into his hat, so what? When people see me do that, they admire the way I share our wealth. It makes you look good."

"You're not upset I beat him to death?" Michael looked at her in disbelief.

The happy times she'd spent with Steve danced across her memory. She pushed down the gut-wrenching despair and just tried to breathe. He'd died for her and now she must be the strong one and see the mission through. There'd be no time to grieve for him now. She swallowed bile and tossed her hair over one shoulder. "Why should I? I don't know him. He played nice music, but do I care if he's dead? No!" She glared at him. "Can I go now? It stinks in here."

To her surprise, he took her hand and led her back to the house, heart pounding so fast Avril thought it might explode from her chest and bounce across the pathway. She drew in deep breaths and met her husband's stride. "You interrupted me. I was watching Mai's lessons."

"I'm glad Mai has settled in so well. She understands us more by the day." Michael gave a satisfied smile. "I'll take her to see my father. He was asking after her just before."

The shock of seeing Steve's battered body made her knees tremble, and she swallowed hard. One wrong move, one reaction, and he'd kill her. She had to get away and take Mai with her. So much depended on this moment. Pressing her lips together, she struggled not to scream and run away. She looked into Michael's dark eyes and suppressed a shudder. His sudden change of mood frightened her more than if he'd hit her again. The taste of blood still coated her tongue and the thought of him taking Mai disturbed her. Michael was in no mood to care for a child. "I'll come with you."

"Not this time." Michael frowned at her. "You look a mess, and it's only two hours until our guests arrive. Go and soak in a tub or whatever it is you do to make yourself presentable. I'll have Mai back in no time at all."

Unable to offer a plausible excuse to prevent Michael taking Mai, she swallowed her protest and stared after him as he collected her from the nursery. The little girl looked over her shoulder at Avril with a confused expression as he led her out the front door and across the lawn to his father's house. Concern gripped Avril's gut at the thought of Viktor and Michael's sudden interest in Vietnamese girls. On face value, most would commend them for assisting the children to find better lives, but the Carlos family only did things that earned them a nice fat profit. Holding back her emotions, she lifted her chin and walked into the nursery as the teacher was collecting her things. "I wonder if you'd have time to wait until Mai returns? I'm happy to pay extra, and cook has a freshly baked cherry pie if you'd like a slice with a coffee while you wait?"

"That would be nice." The teacher placed her books on the table and looked at her. "I see from your eyes that you'd prefer the child doesn't visit your father-in-law. Do you want me to ask Mai when she returns how they treated her?"

Not exactly trusting her but having no choice, Avril nodded. "It would put my mind at rest. My aim is to ensure Mai is happy here and my father-in-law can be a little hard to get along with."

"Well then, I'll stay until she returns." The teacher smiled. "Mai likes you and trusts you, but she misses her family."

There's no future for her here either. Avril nodded. "I know she does, it's difficult losing your family." Trying hard to keep it together, she glanced at her watch. "Oh, look at the time. I have to go and get ready for the dinner tonight. Head down to the kitchen and ask the cook for some pie. I'll drop by the nursery in an hour. Mai should be back by then."

Avril hurried to her room and collapsed on the bed. Tears came and sobs shook her as she cried in silent agony for Steve. His battered face filled her head. He'd suffered incredible torture and yet kept silent to save her life. She gave herself a little shake. If she fell to bits now, he'd have died for nothing. Whatever happened next, she'd bring the cartel to justice if she died trying. Rolling off the bed, she stared at her red eyes. Oh, Lord, Michael would be watching her for any sign of concern and acting normal now would mean he wouldn't be watching her too closely later. If Steve had gotten her message through, she'd have a very slim chance to escape the cartel tonight. She'd confirm her evac with the nurse at the clinic and checked the time. Sighing with relief, she made the call. "Good afternoon. Sorry to call so late. It's Avril Carlos. I'd like to confirm my appointment time, please."

"Midnight, out back of the general store, blue truck with TAUBMAN'S HARDWARE *on the side."*

Avril heaved a sigh of relief. "Thank you."

Not knowing if Michael had bugged her room, she couldn't risk mentioning anything about Steve. She'd deploy her exit plan. After disconnecting, she pushed a few essentials into a backpack for Mai and herself. After counting the cash in her wallet, she hurried downstairs on the pretense of checking the hall again. On the way back, she slipped inside the garage. The sedan Michael had given her as a wedding present but rarely allowed her to drive, was gassed up and ready to go. She dropped the backpack inside and grabbed the keys from the board. Pushing the keys into her pocket, she went back to the house. As soon as the Carloses were fully involved with their guests, she'd take Mai and make a run for it.

It was an hour or so later. Avril had used eyedrops to take the red out of her eyes and applied makeup before heading to the nursery in her bathrobe to find Mai chatting to her teacher. The little girl seemed animated and Avril sat down beside her. She looked at the teacher. "Where has she been?"

"She tells me your husband took her to meet some other children like her. He told her to tell them about her life here with you and how they are safe now." The teacher looked at her with a quizzical expression. "The phrases Mr. Carlos insisted she understand came in useful it seems." She frowned. "From this I assume you have plans for these children?"

Avril nodded and pulled another lie from her hat. She had no choice. "Yes, like our family there are many wealthy people willing to adopt an orphan. My husband contacted the authorities asking permission for a few families to foster these kids. These children Mai mentioned must be who he was referring to. I haven't seen them because I've been busy organizing the dinner for tonight's auction, but I'll ask Michael when he comes home." She held out her hand to Mai. "Come on. I'll take you down for your dinner and then it's a bath, an hour of TV, and off to bed." She led the little girl out of the room and down to the kitchen.

"Oh, there she is." The housekeeper greeted her. "Hello, Mai." She looked up at Avril. "Mr. Carlos asked me to care for her tonight. I have her dinner ready and I'm very happy to look after her and put her to bed. I know what shows she likes to watch."

Avril smiled. "Thank you. She likes you." She kissed Mai on the cheek. "I'll see you soon."

The housekeeper often cared for Mai when Avril was

working and they had gotten along just fine. She went back upstairs to dress and, after making sure everything was running on time, headed for Michael's room to find him wearing a tux and a wide smile. "It's almost seven, I need to go and greet our guests. You look happy. Have you had a few bids already?"

"You could say that." Michael held out his arm and escorted her out of the room and down the stairs. "You don't have to hang around after the dinner. It's a men-only auction—you know, cigars and fine wine. They can get a bit raucous, so my father and I will take it from there. Don't wait up."

The dismissal stung and suspicion crawled over Avril like a poison ivy rash. The gnawing apprehension that something wasn't what it seemed just wouldn't go away. She'd known Michael too long not to recognize he had more on his mind than a wine auction. His eyes had almost lit up with dollar signs. The situation was escalating fast and she couldn't stop him alone. Michael was like an out-of-control freight train. If she got in his way, he'd crush her under his wheels.

EIGHT

Acting like a doting wife and greeting the twelve men as they stepped out of their chauffeur-driven limos had become almost second nature to Avril, but inside she wanted to scream. Her mind conjured all sorts of scenarios. After an hour or so of wine talk, the men moved into the hall. It had been tastefully decorated and the tables were set with white linen tablecloths and the finest silverware. When the men had taken their seats and the help moved around serving the dinner, she took a deep breath and leaned toward Michael. "Mai enjoyed her time with you. She mentioned seeing other children. Are these the ones you've found homes for?"

"How could she have told you?" Michael raised both eyebrows. "She hardly speaks a word of English."

Avril forced her lips into a smile. "Oh, we have a way of communicating and she understands the words you insisted she learn. Did you want her to inform the children they were going to good homes?"

"Something like that." Michael waved a waiter to the table and asked for another bottle of wine. He turned his dark gaze on her. "The children aren't your concern. You're sticking your nose into my father's business and he won't be pleased." His mouth turned down. "And don't get too attached to Mai. It would be a mistake. I've already made plans for her."

Stomach clenching, Avril stared at him. "I thought you'd planned to adopt her."

"No." He barked a laugh. "Only children of my blood will inherit the estate. You'll have one more chance to produce me an heir. I've made arrangements with a fertility clinic to see if they can fix you." His expression went serious. "Let's hope they can for your sake."

Trying not to gag, Avril met his gaze. "Nothing would make me happier than to give you a child, Michael."

They finished their meal. The man seated beside her was sweating profusely and seemed agitated. She ignored him, stood, and leaned to kiss Michael on the cheek. "I'll leave you to your auction."

"I'll have someone drive you back to the house." Michael went to stand.

"No, don't leave your guests. I'll walk." Avril smiled at him. "Nothing can possibly happen to me, and I like to walk in the moonlight."

"Don't wait up. It's going to be a long night." Michael turned back to his guests.

Moving through the hall as swiftly as possible, Avril headed for the back entrance. She pulled open the door and positioned a broom handle to prevent it from closing. She hightailed it back to the main entrance and headed toward the house. The pathways wound between rose gardens and the heady scent would be the only thing she'd miss when she left this place. She hurried inside the house and dashed to her room. Inside, Mai was sound asleep. Avril dressed quickly in black jeans, shirt, and a hoodie. She woke Mai as gently as possible, helped her dress, and tried to explain she needed her to be quiet and that they were off on an adventure. Carrying a pillow and blanket, they left through the mudroom and made their way to the garage. They climbed into the red sports car. She placed the pillow and blanket on the back seat and clicked Mai into the seat belt. She waited for the little girl to settle down. It didn't take long for her to fall to sleep.

Avril checked her watch. The auction should have started by now. Easing out of the car door, she took off at a run, keeping to the shadows around the back of the wine cellar building. After waiting a few seconds to regain her breath, she slipped inside the service door and crept through the passageways, taking the back stairs down to the cellar. The gate had a keypad lock and she used a memorized combination of numbers to gain entrance. She could hear men's voices, laughter, and bidding. The figures were extremely high even for one of the Carlos vintages. She moved through the dusty racks to peer at the group of people in the area set up with chairs, but not one of the men was seated. They were passing young girls around between them as if they were buying kittens. Each girl had a number and Viktor was taking bids. Horrified, Avril swallowed the overwhelming need to spew.

What could she possibly do to stop this happening? She had no weapons, no backup, nothing. Gritting her teeth, she considered her options. Breaking her cover and getting help for these girls was paramount. Michael was not getting away with selling children—not on her watch. She'd have to call it in and then run for her life. She headed back through the passageways and into a utility room to call her handler. After explaining the urgency of the situation, but not wanting to jeopardize the mission, she offered a solution. "The limos will be leaving with the girls. You'll have to pull them over in a routine traffic stop when they leave and take the bidders and their drivers into custody. The auction has just begun, so you'll have time to cover all roads leading from here. Just make sure they don't call Michael and give him a heads-up. You'll need to keep them silent until the raid. You can't delay. You must hit them before they discover I'm missing. I'm leaving for the evac point now." She disconnected and deleted the call log. It had become a habit.

Pushing the phone inside her pocket, she moved swiftly along the passageways. When she turned the corner to the back entrance, she ran slap bang into Michael. She gaped at him but said nothing. Whatever happened, before this night was out the girls would be safe and he'd be arrested. She'd won, and if he killed her, it was worth it.

"So now you know about my latest enterprise. Like wine, it is something I can enjoy. Snooping around isn't your style, Avril. Are you jealous or was it because I didn't want to keep Mai? Don't you understand that I don't care what you think? You promised to obey me and I'll see that you do." Michael slapped her hard. "She is worth her weight in gold. I already have bids for her."

Anger rising, Avril took the slap and just stared at him. This defiance made him angry and he backhanded her again. Black spots danced across her vision and pain radiated through her brain, but she refused to look away from him. She had to outwit this monster and get away to save Mai. Squeezing her hands into fists, she shook her head. "Why are you doing this? They're only little kids."

"Those girls pay for your fine clothes and the house you live in. This is what my father calls 'value-adding'." Michael grinned. "We can keep Mai but she won't be sleeping in your room anymore. She'll become a pet for me and my father... and maybe a few of my bodyguards."

Avril swallowed blood and lifted her chin. His bodyguard was smiling at her. Not a big man, because big men made Michael look small, he carried a weapon in a shoulder holster under his jacket. "What do you want me to say, Michael?"

"You're a strange one." Michael bent to look into her eyes. "You don't react like any woman I know." He grabbed her by the arm and dragged her out the door. "Do you have any feelings at all? Let's see if this will get a reaction out of you."

Dragged behind him as Michael strode along the back wall of the building and to the pergola foundations, Avril staggered trying to keep her balance. The smell of death lingered like a sickening fog and she noticed another hole beside a pile of fresh earth. In the light of the full moon, she caught sight of a child soaked in blood. She dug in her heels and gaped at him. "What have you done?"

"This is what happens to those who don't cooperate." Michael spun her around to face him. "It's business and our clients only want the best." A slow smile spread across his face. "Welcome to my world. You have a choice, just like the kids: cooperate or die."

Avril swallowed the bile in her mouth and stared at him. Could she outsmart him one more time? "I'm not stupid. I know you kill people. I've always liked your bad-boy image. That's why I married you." She straightened. Her face was still stinging from his blow. "Now can I go? I'm tired."

"If you can get back to the house before Gus catches you, sure, but if not, you'll be joining the kid in the hole." He dropped her arm and held both his hands up. "I'll even count to three. One..."

Avril sprinted, but she could hear the heavy footsteps pounding behind her. In fear of her life, she bolted for the garage, tearing across the lawns and jumping over gardens. Gus moved faster than she'd expected and he was close behind her when she made it into the garage. Vaulting onto a workbench, she grabbed a heavy wrench from the tools set out on the wall and took aim. As Gus ran by, she swung it like a baseball bat at his head. The impact vibrated up her arms and into her jaw. His momentum made him stagger, arms reaching for her, and then he dropped like a stone. Not wasting any time, she pulled out her keys and ran to her vehicle. Hands trembling, she opened the door and slid behind the wheel. Glancing over one shoulder to check that Mai was still asleep, she started the engine. It took every ounce of patience to drive the sports car slowly toward the gate. The sound of the powerful engine could raise the dead if she panicked and hit the gas. The massive iron gates swung open so darn slowly, she wanted to scream. Checking her rearview mirror for anyone watching her, she eased the car through the space and headed off the estate. Once she hit the interstate, she took off at high speed. Using the Bluetooth app on her car, she called her handler. She fumbled over her identity check and was desperate by the time his voice came through the speaker. "Get me the hell out of here. I'm on the interstate heading north. Red Lamborghini."

"Keep driving. I have your position. We'll send a chopper to intercept."

Gripping the wheel, Avril pushed her foot to the floor. The magnificent car responded and they flashed passed vehicles effortlessly. "I have a little girl with me. I'm coming in hot. Keep the cops off my tail. It's only a matter of time before the cartel will be chasing me."

"Copy that. Don't worry. Help is on the way. We're going to take the cartel down, Avril, and those pedophiles buying up kids. It will be the biggest bust in history. You'll be famous."

Avril didn't want to be famous. She just wanted to be safe.

NINE

It had been hard to hand over Mai to child protection, but good news came within the day that they had located her family. Her father, a diplomat, had reported her missing from school and with his assistance all the stolen children would be returned to their families. The raid on the Carlos Winery that night was all over the media. With the drug-processing plant exposed and after discovering Michael Carlos's extensive video brochure of prospective children for sale, Viktor and Michael, along with his henchmen, were in the process of trying to plea-bargain their way out of jail. It would never happen. Avril would stand as the state's evidence against them. Her testimony, both physical and verbal, would see them rot in jail.

The funeral of Steve Breuer had left her limp and depressed. She'd undergone so many psych tests that she thought they'd send her insane. Restricted to a desk job and watched like a hawk, she completed mundane tasks. Burly guards escorted her everywhere. She'd not been able to live at home and US Marshals had moved her every few days. Concern the cartel would get to her before the trial put her nerves on edge, and she had the awful feeling someone was watching her from every shadow or doorway. The months that went by before the trials of Viktor and Michael Carlos seemed to drag like years. Then the news came that Michael had fallen in the shower and accidentally cut his throat. It seemed that some of the other prisoners had a problem with men who used children as a commodity. That left Viktor Carlos and a long list of his relatives, all who'd been involved in his crime empire, out for her blood. The moment she stepped onto the stand, she'd have a target on her back for the rest of her life.

All eyes followed Avril as she took the stand to give her evidence to a hushed, humid courtroom. As the prosecution outlined its case and asked her questions, the tension could be cut with a knife. As the story unfolded of what she'd endured and witnessed, reporters stared at her openmouthed. The temperature inside the room seemed to be climbing by the minute. Heart pounding under the disgusted gaze of Viktor Carlos, she sipped from a glass of water between the questions. The air conditioner rattled, pouring out a pathetic whisper of cool air into the stifling heat. The room stank of sweat, and perspiration ran down her back in trickles. After she'd detailed everything she'd witnessed in her time undercover, Viktor Carlos's defense team tore her reputation to shreds. She remained calm and refused to allow him to upset her, although the attorney painted her as a liar. She kept to the truth and the jury listened intently. They examined the mountain of evidence, including her photographs, and after four days of deliberation made the right decision to convict Viktor Carlos. His cohorts fell like bowling pins after him, but Avril would never forget the moment before they led Viktor Carlos away after sentencing.

"You." Viktor Carlos pointed at Avril, his eyes blazing with hatred. "Look at me, bitch. I'm coming for you. You can't hide from me. Even when I'm dead, my blood will find you. You'll never be safe."

Shaken, Avril stared after him as he shuffled away in orange coveralls and chains, surrounded by guards. The DA walked up to her and narrowed his gaze. "I'm afraid you have a target on your back and no doubt there's a massive bounty on your head."

Avril swallowed hard. "It was worth it. He'll never walk free again. I'm not scared of him."

"You should be." The DA's shoulders drooped. "The cartel has fingers everywhere. We'll try to get them all, but the odds are someone will be out there just waiting to claim a reward. I suggest you listen to the offer of witness protection that's coming your way. You don't have anyone, do you? No family or boyfriend to keep you here?"

Chewing on her bottom lip, Avril shook her head. "Witness protection? Are you joking? Do you expect me to give up my career, everything I've worked for? What do you expect me to do? How can I earn a living? I'm only interested in law enforcement."

"If you don't go into hiding, you won't last a month." The DA urged her out of the courtroom and through the barrage of media. "Go with the US Marshals and listen to what they have to say. If you want to live, it's the only choice. It's been nice knowing you, Avril." He smiled and disappeared into the crowd.

Devastated, she turned and walked toward the two US Marshals waiting to escort her and sighed. "Okay, let's go."

As they whisked her away to an unknown destination, the world came tumbling down around her. Emotions poured over her. She'd lost everything. It was as if she'd committed the crimes and was being punished. Her years of training, her hopes and dreams, shattered in seconds. What would happen to her? She thought of the sacrifice Steve had given to protect her. Beaten to a pulp, he'd kept her safe. How many men would do that? She owed him to keep going and she vowed then and there to remain in law enforcement no matter what the cost. The bad guys would not win on her watch, and she'd do whatever it took to honor Steve's sacrifice.

The vehicle turned into a deep underground garage and stopped in an allotted space. Avril slid from the back seat and walked beside the two men down long white passageways and into a room. Behind the desk sat a man. The smell of sweat and stale aftershave greeted her and the man stood and waved her to a chair. He didn't introduce himself and had an expression cast in stone. She took the offered seat. "I've spoken to the DA about the threat from the cartel. What's the deal?"

"There is only one option Agent Parker." He sat and faced her across the desk. "You must go into witness protection. Usually by the time you walk into my office, it's a done deal. You take what we offer as it's the best option available, but we've been given instructions to discuss various possibilities with you."

Hackles raised, Avril snorted in disgust. "I'm not a drug dealer or criminal ratting on a member of his gang. I'm a federal agent who gave two years of my life to bring down a billion-dollar drug syndicate and child-smuggling racket." She dug one finger into the table. "I don't want to go into witness protection but if I have no choice, then I'm going somewhere I like, that's for sure."

"We have a few places that might suit you." The man wearing the badge sounded like a car salesman. "Small towns, where you could get by working in a truck stop or in one of the restaurants. The idea is to keep a low profile and not draw attention to yourself." He went on, describing a list of mundane, boring examples of a new life.

Wanting to roll her eyes, Avril listened but shook her head. Nothing he had said convinced her to accept his offer. "I'm not hiding. I want a life. I'm owed a life for what I've suffered over the last two years. I'm a trained law enforcement officer. I'm sure as hell not waiting tables. I did that working through college and I worked my butt off to make the grade. I obviously need to be able to protect myself, so I want to at least live in a place where I can legally carry a weapon."

"That's not possible." He clasped his hands on the table in front of him and raised both eyebrows. "What you're suggesting would take extensive plastic surgery—a complete makeover. I'd need to get permission from way above my paygrade to authorize that, Agent Parker."

Avril shrugged and leaned back in her chair. "I've all the time in the world." She met his gaze. "The media will have a field day if one of Viktor Carlos's men takes me down. I'm willing to do whatever it takes to change my appearance, but I'm not cowering from that monster for the rest of my life. Either I'll find work in law enforcement or work toward being elected as a city counselor, whatever. I'm planning on making a noise about spousal abuse. No woman should have to go through what I did and so many people just don't want to get involved. I'm going to change that attitude if it's the last thing I do."

"That's very brave of you and it will be a tough path to follow. Now, if you'll go with my men outside, there's a break-room just down the hall." He stood and waved her toward the door. "I'll make a few calls and see what I can do."

It was then Avril discovered that US Marshals didn't have a whole lot to say. They directed her to the room and left her to use the coffee machine, help herself to a few wrapped cookies, and spend time in the bathroom. In contrast to the courthouse, this room was stark, cold, and only the smell of coffee lingered. Goosebumps prickled on her arms as she sat for over an hour staring at the bare walls, her mind racing with the implications of being in witness protection. All the while, the two men standing outside the door remained motionless. No one was getting near her. She pondered a future outside the DEA. Being an only child, she'd been lonely, and then when fate had handed her the final blow by taking her parents, joining the FBI had been her only solace. It had been her life. All the friends she'd made had become a surrogate family. The idea of being completely alone concerned her. Being part of a team had been her life for so long. It was like being cast out without one soul to go to for advice or even to visit. She envisioned a lonely existence because, in truth, she'd never be able to trust anyone again. The abuse she suffered under Michael's hands had scarred her. Being powerless to fight back, had given her a very up-front and personal insight to spousal abuse. One thing was for sure: She'd never allow a man to strike her again. She'd fight back and scream her protests to the powers that be to stop it from happening to others. Trying not to wallow in self-pity, she looked at the positives. At least she'd taken down the kingpin of a drug-manufacturing cartel and saved millions of lives by stopping the poison from getting to the streets.

Eventually, the word came for her to return to the small office. She sat down and waited for the man across the desk to speak. After he said nothing but just stared at his computer screen, she cleared her throat. "Have you come up with a solution?"

The man turned to face her and raised his gray eyebrows. He shrugged. "I can't guarantee this will work and I must stress that once you accept the placement, you'll be on your own. Any interference from us will bring attention to you. The arms of the cartel are endless. It was a family business and you can be assured Viktor Carlos will always have someone out there willing to serve their own type of justice. A vendetta is for life and you should be aware you've placed yourself in a very dangerous position."

Trying to keep her cool, Avril stared at him in disbelief. "The DEA placed me in this position. I was doing my job and now you're saying I'm the one on death row. Give me a break. Is this the thanks I get for my service?"

"The powers that be will be watching over you, but at a distance." He leaned forward a little as if sharing a confidence. "I'm not ruling out that assistance may be supplied in the future, perhaps someone in the same situation as you, but it will be up to you initially to create a new life for yourself. We figure changing you enough so you can hide in plain sight would give you the best opportunity to work in your chosen field... as in law enforcement, but at a different level."

The tension in Avril's jaw relaxed a little. "Go on."

"You're owed a debt of gratitude—there's no disputing that —but the only place I can suggest is a backwoods town in Montana. A place by the name of Black Rock Falls." He turned around his screen to display a picturesque town with a back-drop of mountains and pine trees. Blue sky stretched out forever. It looked like heaven. He raised both eyebrows. "The sheriff died recently and the town is being run by an acting sheriff, but he's old and the townsfolk will be electing someone more suitable. But so far there are no candidates. The council elections are next November. That would give us time to change your appearance and set up a cover story as a cop who needs a break from city life. You're smart and resourceful. If you get the townsfolk behind you, you might get elected. Worse case, if you lose the election, they'll employ you as a deputy. From there, you would have a chance to put yourself forward in the elections, but that's a wait if you don't make it the first time." He gave her a long look. "It's a start, but it's up to you. Do you figure you can make it work?"

Avril stared at him in disbelief. "You honestly believe they'd accept a woman as sheriff? You're crazy."

"Things are changing. Women have loud voices and you'll be going there as an experienced big-city cop. That goes a long way in a small town. We'll give you creds as a gold-shield detec-tive. That will gain you a ton of respect." He smiled at her. "It's a pretty place. Low crime rate and big open spaces. Blue skies that stretch forever and a growing community. It will be the last place the cartel will look for you. You'll have the chance for a normal life. We'll make sure you know everything about the town and its laws. You'll slide in like a local. What do you say?"

Thinking of the ten million she'd stashed in an offshore account waiting for her, she nodded. That sort of money could keep her comfortable for life. As they couldn't change her DNA, fingerprints, or eyes, she'd always be under constant threat of discovery. But who would look for her out of Black Rock Falls? She met his gaze. "Okay, I'll do it."

TEN

The US Marshals had taken Avril to a secure facility and hadn't given her location. She had no phone or connection with the outside world apart from a US Marshal, a doctor, and a couple of nurses who refused to talk about anything but the weather. She'd undergone extensive facial reconstruction and surgeries to change her body shape, including breast implants. Not the huge ones, just enough to take her from flat chested to what she'd consider normal. She let out a cheer when at last they gave her the luxury of a TV.

The constant flow of nurses moving in and out of the room drove her crazy. All she wanted to do was to relax and watch the news. It was the only respite from the long days holed up in the same room. She'd had no contact with the US Marshals about the plans for her future. She picked up the TV remote and watched the familiar anchorman talk about politics. Then without warning an image of her flashed on the screen followed by a burned-out shell of a boat. Her world tilted sideways as the newsreader's voice slammed into her.

"Avril Parker, the DEA agent responsible for the arrest and

prosecution of underworld kingpin Viktor Carlos was found dead after the speedboat she was traveling in caught fire and exploded..."

The rest of his words became a jumbled mess of nonsense. Shocked into disbelief, she gaped at the screen trembling. In a few seconds, her life had been snatched away from her and just as quickly she'd be forgotten.

Why hadn't anyone explained this to her? The shock sent the hospital monitors into overdrive. Nurses came running and moments later she sunk into a drug-induced sleep.

Now legally dead, she hung in limbo for three long days before the US Marshal arrived to explain.

"It was the best thing to do." The US Marshal shrugged. "The cartel might buy it. They might not, but it will give you the best chance of survival."

Avril looked up at him from her hospital bed. "So, who am I now?"

"We've chosen the name Jenna Alton." He gave her a satisfied smile. "It was discussed at length and was the most popular choice."

Unconvinced, Avril stared at him. "Jenna Alton? I don't look like a Jenna." She wrinkled her nose and gasped at the sudden wave of pain from her surgery. For heaven's sake, she had no sense of smell and hadn't been able to breathe properly for over a week. "Can't I have something else? Say, something closer to my real name. What about April?"

"No, that's the name we've chosen for you. The paperwork is already underway. When the bandages come off and you dye your hair black, the name will suit you. That's your name from today, so get used to it, Jenna." He sighed. "It fits well in Montana. How are you going with studying the local laws and customs?"

"It's a work in progress." Puffing out a sigh of resignation,

Jenna touched the bandages covering her face and winced. She didn't do lying in bed all day and was forever slipping out of bed to stare out of the small window. But if she moved around too much, the doctor came in and gave her a shot. Being controlled in such a way did nothing for her mood. "I hope you're right. The bandages come off today and I get to see Jenna Alton." She lifted her gaze back to him. "Have I taken the identity of a dead woman?"

"Nope." The marshal sat down in the chair beside the bed. "You'll be supplied with all the documentation you require. When you're ready to leave here, we'll escort you to the airport and then you're on your own. There'll be a vehicle waiting for you in the airport parking lot and a place to stay that's paid up for three months. You'll have a bank account with a decent balance to cover you until you get a job. There'll be no checking in, no contact with the department. You'll be virtually alone, but in truth we'll keep an eye on you from afar." He smiled. "It's all up to you now, Jenna. Study hard and get well. You have six months to get back into shape and then we're setting you free. Good luck." He stood and walked out the door.

Suddenly feeling very alone, Jenna stared after him. "I'm going to need it."

Later in the day the doctor came and removed the bandages. He looked at her critically. It was the look doctors gave people that hid all their real feelings, and Jenna's stomach rolled. She lifted her chin. "Well, do I look like Frankenstein's monster?"

"No, you look really good. Younger, of course. I'd place you at around twenty-two. Your eyebrows are a little higher and the nose a little shorter. I've lifted your eyes in the corners to give them a slightly different tilt. I can assure you, once the swelling has gone down, and the hairdresser has come by to add the finishing touches, you'll be happy. No one will recognize you now." He indicated to the bathroom. "Go take a look."

Jenna slipped from the bed and padded barefoot to the bathroom. She took a deep breath and peered at her reflection. A stranger looked back at her. Not even her eyes were the same. Although, she had to admit, she liked the new person. The doctor had turned back the years and the worry lines had vanished. Her skin looked refreshed and younger. All the scars on her face where Michael had hit her were gone. Each time she'd looked into the mirror, they'd been a constant reminder of his power over her. Now with the scars gone, maybe one day, she'd forget he'd ever existed. She shuddered. No, she'd never forget how she'd suffered by his hand, helpless to fight back. She stared at the new, confidant person standing before her. Tough and resilient, this woman could stand and fight alone if needs be. No, Jenna Alton would never allow a man to hit her and get away with it. She'd fight back whatever the cost. She'd take the seven years the doctor had taken from her appearance and make good use of them. Heading back into the room, she smiled at the doctor. "I kinda like Jenna Alton, but I'm not sure if I can handle not being blonde. The upkeep will be murder."

"We're thinking shoulder-length black. The current swept-up long blonde style is too much like your old life. It's almost a signature of how you looked before. Think less high-class fashion and more country. You'll be living with mountain men and miners. If you arrive looking like a city girl, they'll get suspicious and you'll be treated like an outsider." He glanced at her hands. "Trim the nails. No polish. You're not undercover. I'm to inform you that someone will drop by as soon as you're healed to start training you. You'll need to get your hand-to-hand combat skills back to normal. Two years undercover has made you soft. You'll be out on the rifle range, getting your eye back in. They want to make sure of your proficiency over a wide range of weapons. They want you in top condition before they let you go. Think of it as a mission, and if you succeed, the payoff is a great new life. It's a nice town filled with good people, Jenna. They need someone like you. Go and help them."

Mind spinning with the possibilities and pitfalls, Jenna nodded. "Okay, not that I have any choice, but I'll give it my best shot."

ELEVEN

The weeks of training had been torture. Jenna had grown weak during her recovery and the fifty-or-so-year-old man of steel with features carved out of stone sent to retrain her was relentless. He'd changed her body shape completely. Building muscle had given her a sculpted appearance that enhanced her. Not too much muscle, but enough to round her bottom and give her the strong thighs she'd always admired on female athletes. Her strength had increased substantially and she'd gained techniques for defending herself she hadn't learned at Quantico. After Jenna bid farewell to the medical team and actually got a flash of a smile from her trainer, a US Marshal had seen her onto a flight to Black Rock Falls. The so-called small backwoods town had an airport, a large hospital, a college, and everything in between, ice hockey teams, football teams, and a place for the rodeo circuit. In fact, it seemed the town was not only prosperous but expanding at an incredible rate and was a well-known tourist destination. From the window of the aircraft, the scenery had taken her breath away. Tall black mountains dusted with snow rose up around the town like a circle of protection, and below, pine trees covered the terrain as far as the eye could see. Waterfalls, rivers, and lakes spread out in abundance, glistening under an endless azure blue sky. The sight filled her with a calmness she'd never experienced before. Black Rock Falls called to her as if it was her special place. She had the strangest feeling of going home.

From the moment she left the airport and headed for the parking lot to search for the rental they'd supplied for her, the scent of the forest caressed her on a light breeze. She could sense the lingering taste of winter and the familiar smell of snow. Her many skiing holidays came back in a rush of memories. She'd so loved the mountains and here they surrounded her in a protective hug. Swallowing the lump in her throat, she followed the signposts into town. It was bigger than she expected. After pulling over to add the address of the real estate office on Main to the GPS, she followed the instructions. She needed to drop by to pick up the keys to the rental house in town. The real estate office stood out with its slightly tattered bunting waving in the breeze and she pulled to the curb and climbed out. Exhausted from the flight, she leaned against the vehicle, and her attention went straight to a welcoming sign depicting a slice of steaming apple pie on a red plaid plate and the name AUNT BETTY'S CAFÉ.

The smell of good coffee and baking drifted toward her on the air. As if pulled by a magnet, she crossed the road and went inside. A long glass counter displayed pies and other delicious treats. Behind on the wall were glossy posters of every meal on offer and to one side of the counter hung a blackboard with the day's specials. The diner was bigger than she expected and the majority of seats were already taken. She glanced around at the spotless tables, all with red and white plaid tablecloths, surrounded by wooden chairs with seats worn down from many visitors. To her surprise, the customers looked at her and smiled. She headed for the counter and sighed in delight. The delicious aromas pouring out from the kitchen had her hooked in an instant. Only excellent food smelled that good. She smiled at a young woman with the nameplate SUSIE.

"How can I help you?" Susie gave her a bright smile. "New in town?"

Jenna nodded. "I just arrived and I'm here to stay." She glanced at the display of photographs of the many items on offer. "I'm famished. What do you suggest?"

"Well, everything is good. We have fresh bagels and the best peach pie in the state."

Mouth watering in anticipation, Jenna nodded. "Bagel and cream cheese, and I'll have a slice of that pie. Coffee as well, please."

"Go and make yourself at home. I'll have it ready before you know it." Susie disappeared out back.

Jenna looked for an empty table just as an old deputy walked into the café and headed for a seat toward the back. She glanced at him and smiled. "Would you be Deputy Walters?"

"That would be me." The old man smiled at her. "Can I be of any assistance, ma'am?"

The lie would begin with this man and Jenna hoped she had her story straight. "I've just arrived in town. I was going to drop by the sheriff's office in the morning. I'm Jenna Alton. I was a detective out of Baltimore. I asked my captain to contact the sheriff here. I'm looking for work in law enforcement."

"Well, I wasn't expecting someone so young." Walters eyed her critically. "Your boss said you're a hotshot gold-shield detective. Why did you leave?"

"I'm almost thirty and I left because of a messy relationship breakup." She sighed. "I needed to get a long way away and make a fresh start and I chose this town."

"Oh, I'm so sorry." Walters leaned back in his seat as Susie arrived with her meal and poured coffee for her and Walters.

"Oh, I see you two know each other." Susie smiled at Walters. "The usual?"

"Yeah, thanks, Susie." Walters waited a beat and looked at Jenna. "Do you mind me sitting here with you for a time?"

Jenna shook her head. "Not at all." She cleared her throat. "Is there any work available?"

"There sure is." Walters nodded his head wisely. "I need help. Since the sheriff died, I've been on my lonesome. Can you drop by the sheriff's office in the morning? I'm acting sheriff and can swear you in as a deputy, but as you're new in town I should take you over to meet Mayor Rockford. I figure you'll fit into this town just fine."

Interested, Jenna nibbled at her bagel. "Okay. That sounds perfect."

"As a deputy, you'll get to know the townsfolk firsthand." He gave her a slow smile. "Truth is, we need a sheriff. I'm close to retirement and my arthritis is so bad I couldn't chase down anyone if my life depended on it. And my eyes aren't so good either. We need new blood, and with your experience, once the townsfolk get to know you and you do a bit of campaigning, they'll vote you in as sheriff. You'll need to get your name down before the closing date and then you'll have time to campaign. I'll walk you through the process in the morning."

Jenna met his gaze. "Do you really think they'd elect a woman sheriff?"

"I don't see why not." He chuckled. "We'll likely have the usual candidates for you to go against. They try every year, but the townsfolk have issues with all of them. You'd have a good chance. No one here has your track record. You're an experienced detective from the big city and people want someone to keep them safe. Things are changing and the women in this town want a voice. You might just be that voice, Jenna Alton."

Jenna ate and thought it over as Deputy Walkers finished a bowl of chili. She glanced at him over the edge of the bottomless cup of coffee. No sooner had she finished her cup than a pot of coffee arrived on the table with more fixings. She took a breath. "So, what are the main problems in town?"

"Before the sheriff died, he had a few calls, mostly from neighbors complaining that they heard screams and fights." He gave her a long look. "I went out a few times and spoke to the people involved. Heck, I could see the women had suffered a beating but not one of them would say a word against their husbands." He shrugged. "I took them to one side and told them if they pressed charges, their husbands would be fined or maybe go to jail for a time, but not one of them would cooperate."

A shiver went down Jenna's spine. She'd had firsthand knowledge of how it felt to be helpless and vulnerable. If a woman in the same situation had children, it would be worse. With nowhere to go and a husband hell-bent on revenge, no one would be willing to press charges. She shook her head. "I'm not surprised. The potential consequences of bashing your partner are weak in this state. I mean with the first offense set at twenty-four hours to one year in jail and a fine from as little as one hundred dollars to a maximum of one thousand for the first offense, that's hardly a deterrent, is it?" She rubbed her temples. "Do any of the victims apply for a protective order?"

"No, not a one." Walters smiled at her. "See you'd be perfect for the job of sheriff. You know the law and would be a voice for the women in town. A beaten woman often refuses to confide in a male officer."

Jenna lifted her chin. "Men or women can both suffer abuse. For me it would make no difference, same as color or religion. I'm not biased. I see everyone as a person with the same rights." She leaned back in her chair and looked at him. "But I'm a stickler for the law. No one would slide under the radar and I sure as hell would never be bribed."

"Sounds to me like we've found our sheriff." Walters chuckled. "Is there anything I can do to help you settle in?"

Jenna shook her head. "Nope, I'm good for now. I'll go pick

up the keys to my house and then come back into town to get a few things from the store." She stood and dropped some bills on the table. "I'll see you in the morning and you can bring me up to speed. Thanks for your help. It's been nice meeting you, Deputy." She headed for the door.

TWELVE

Jenna gave Susie a wave as she left Aunt Betty's Café and stopped for a second to take in her surroundings. It was a very interesting town, with plenty of stores, a bank, a general store, a surf-and-turf diner. She'd driven past the local newspaper office and had made out signs for hardware, produce, and a beauty parlor. The townhall was an impressive building and she noticed a sign pointing to a library. It would take her a while, but she'd explore and find out what else the town had to offer.

As she headed back to the real estate office, she passed a faded sign advertising a rodeo and another one peeling at the edges reminding people of the Halloween Festival. But her eyes moved to the notice about the upcoming council elections. She had time to get her name down but she'd have to move fast. Pausing at the display of houses for sale in the real estate's window, her attention riveted on an interesting property. The huge ranch house was her dream home and the property was manageable at one hundred acres. It had a large barn, stables, a corral, and a separate cottage. Fully fenced and surrounded by open lowlands and woods, it looked like an ideal hideaway. She smiled at the price. It wouldn't make a dent in her bank account.

Taking a mental note of the property name, she pushed open the door and into a wall of cigar smoke. She pressed one hand to her nose and met the gaze of an older man, sitting in front of a computer screen behind the desk. "Mr. Davis?"

"That would be me." Davis peered at her over his glasses. "I'm assuming you're Jenna Alton? I have your keys right here." He pulled open a drawer and dropped a bunch of keys on the desk. "There's some paperwork to sign. You're paid up for three months. How long are you planning on staying in town?"

Jenna stared at the cigar smoking in an ashtray on the desk. "Forever, I hope. The rental will be short term. I'm interested in purchasing a property. Could we speak outside? I'm afraid the smell of your cigar makes me sick."

"Oh, yeah... fine." He extinguished the cigar and stood. "Is there something in the window that's caught your eye?"

Pulling open the door and gulping fresh air, Jenna nodded. "Yeah, the O'Reilly Ranch. What can you tell me about it? What condition is it in?"

"The cottage was the first building on the property and built over one hundred years ago, followed by the ranch house." Davis leaned against the side of the red brick building, his expression animated. "It was fully renovated two years ago and hasn't been lived in since. There's power, water, and a generator."

A sudden wave of concern hit Jenna. "Why wasn't it lived in and why hasn't it been sold before now? Is there a problem?"

"Not concerning that property, no, but the surrounding land borders part of the Old Mitcham Ranch. It's not next door. There's a property between the O'Reilly Ranch and the snow-plow guy. He's lived there, right next door for ten years, no problem at all. The Old Mitcham Ranch is said to be cursed. Bad things seem to happen there. The kids go there on

Halloween to scare themselves. They say you can hear a hanged man swinging in the barn. The legend is that Mitcham took his own life after his wife was murdered and he haunts the barn." He cleared his throat. "Stories like that put people off buying a property, which is reflected in the price, but the previous owners never had a problem. They raised two kids and then renovated the property to sell it. They moved to California to be close to their grandchildren."

Frowning, Jenna considered the situation. The house intrigued her. "So, no one died there?"

"Not that I'm aware." Davis opened his hands wide. "It's a beautiful house, big enough to raise ten kids, all new appliances. Plenty of room to spread out and a cellar that goes the entire footprint of the house. The possibilities are endless." He sighed. "The views spread to the mountains on one side and across the lowlands on the other. There's good fishing at the river not five minutes' drive away."

It sounded too good to be true. Jenna stared at the picture of the house and it called to her. She turned to Davis. "Can you take me out and show me... now?" She lifted her chin. "If I like it, we'll do a deal today. I'm a cash buyer. Whatever, I plan to buy a place here. I'll be staying at the rental until I find a suitable house and the paperwork and payment go through."

"I have a few places I can show you. I'll grab the keys and lock up." He hurried inside and was back in less than a minute.

They drove through town, Davis talking like a tour guide, pointing out the best stores for this and that and local attractions. Jenna kept a close eye on the direction they were heading. They drove straight through town, turned left onto a highway, and continued for about ten minutes before passing a group of buildings, another left turn, and then straight ahead. The scenery took Jenna's breath away. To one side she made out the mountains in the distance, with pine trees marching up the slopes. To the other the lowland spread out, the long grass moving in the wind like an ocean. Flowers of every description spotted the landscape with color.

They stopped at a wide gate with a white arch above displaying a bull's skull, and Davis climbed out and opened the padlock. The gate opened with a whine and he strode back to the truck, and they followed the driveway through a wooded area and out to about half an acre of open space. The house was magnificent, a typical old ranch house with a porch. Jenna climbed out and turned in a full circle taking it all in. She inhaled the sweet air and looked at Davis. "Let's see inside."

The ranch house was just as he'd said, freshly painted, the wooden floors glossy, and the kitchen huge. Jenna walked around absorbing the atmosphere. She had a second sense when it came to danger, but this house made her feel welcome. After exploring the rooms, and liking what she'd seen, she headed outside, scanning the perimeter. "I see they've sectioned off the land. I assume they ran livestock?"

"Horses." Davis puffed along behind her. "The stables are in top condition. The corral maybe needs some attention but not much."

Impressed, Jenna turned around again and sighed. She couldn't have ever imagined anything so perfect. Forget any curses, the mind-blowing beauty surrounded her in a warm welcome, to be sure, but the ever-present concern of someone finding her spoiled her delight. Walking back and forth, she mapped out a wide area around the house and buildings. It would be unlikely she'd ever use the land for livestock, and over the past two years, it had returned to its natural state. She could easily erect a high perimeter fence around the house, to prevent unwelcome visitors or perhaps a less noticeable boundary alarm and an electric gate. It would give her enough space for herself, and maybe she'd use the remainder of the land for pastureland but she liked the natural state. It added to the peace. A CCTV display and a good security system were all possible. She'd make it safe. "Okay, show me the cottage and barn."

The cottage was the size of a regular three-bedroom house in town. It had its own fenced yard and was delightful. Obviously built by the pioneer who first owned the land way back when, it too had extensive renovations and was fresh and clean... well, a little dusty like the house, but nothing a mop and bucket wouldn't fix. She moved to the barn. It had an impressive stable, hayloft, and housed the generator. The cellar was huge and she could convert half of it into a safe room. As money wasn't a problem, she'd be able to make this property secure and it was far enough away from anyone to worry about snooping neighbors. She'd remain in town, select her furniture, and then move in when everything was completed.

Smiling, she turned to look at Davis. "I like it. Take me back to your office and we'll make a deal."

When Jenna offered a price, subject to a house inspection, Davis accepted it by rubbing his hands together and smiling. He'd arrange for the inspection to be carried out at once, which surprised her, but work was slow in town right now. She needed someone to oversee the legalities and discovered there was only one available lawyer in town, James Stone, a defense lawyer, who she found had his hand in every pie and would for a substantial fee oversee the transfer of the deed. After Davis made a call, she walked across the road and a woman at the front desk ushered her into James Stone's office.

"Miss Alton, welcome to Black Rock Falls." James Stone, a handsome man in his thirties, flashed her a white smile.

From his attire, he preferred the expensive brand names and she recognized an expensive cologne. His gaze raked her with undisguised admiration and heat filled Jenna's cheeks. "Thank you. It looks like a nice place to live."

"It's a good place to hide." Stone's lips curled up at the edges. "We've more criminals hiding off the grid in the forest than most towns hereabouts, but they keep out of sight. Do you have a dark past? If so, I'm here if you need me." He leaned forward. "You can say anything you like to me, Jenna. As a client, we have confidentiality."

Dumbfounded, Jenna stared into his dark eyes. Not friendly eyes, they had an unreadability about them, maybe something he'd perfected as a defense lawyer. "Well, Mr. Stone, I honestly hope I'll never need your defense expertise. I feel we might be knocking heads, if I get the job I'm applying for in the morning."

"And what is that?" He gave her a slow smile. "Not a prosecutor I hope." He chuckled.

Jenna leaned back in her chair. This guy was so smooth, obviously well educated, which made her wonder why he'd decided to live in a small backwoods Montana town. He came over as a big-city lawyer and she doubted he'd make his fortune here. "I'm a cop—well, let's say I retired from the police force and decided to apply for the position of deputy. I don't have any skeletons in my closet. I had a failed relationship and wanted a new start is all. I'm not hiding. I'm going to be out in plain sight."

"You're very young to have retired." He twirled a pen in his fingers and looked closely at her. "It must have been some breakup." He seemed to shake himself. "Okay let's get down to business. Mr. Davis will send over the paperwork as soon as the inspection is completed and you're satisfied. When you want to proceed, have the funds transferred so we can get the paperwork moving. I'll need a retainer and I'll file everything you need. It usually takes about six weeks, but things are slow in town right now, so maybe sooner." He pulled out a document and pushed it across the table. "This is my permission to proceed on your behalf and my retainer. Give me your details, sign both copies, and take one. You can pay by check or card. See the woman on the front desk."

Jenna nodded, completed the documents, and stood. "Thanks. If the inspection comes back clean, I'll transfer the cash today."

"I'll be in touch." Stone stood and shook her hand.

Once she'd arranged the payment for his retainer, she spent some time in town. She went back to Aunt Betty's Café and had a long conversation with Susie about the town. Susie Hartwig was a font of information and gave her names of suitable contractors along with phone numbers. She spent a happy hour or so immersed in the delicious aromas of fresh baking, drinking coffee, and sampling a cherry pie straight from the oven. She'd found paradise in a diner in the middle of nowhere. The house would fly through the inspection. She'd taken a good look around and it appeared as solid as a rock. The only problem would be getting the contractors to make the changes and arrange for furnishings within three months. To her surprise, she'd either hit on a slow day or Black Rock Falls was a walk-in, walk-out kind of town. Everyone she'd needed was available and could start work the moment she gave them the go-ahead.

* * *

When the call came from the man inspecting the property, she listened with interest to his report. He'd picked out a few minor things. A few roof shingles needed replacing and he'd suggested a new furnace, but apart from that the house was good to go. She called James Stone and instructed him to proceed. Excitement made her burst out in laughter as she headed for the bank. Once inside, she introduced herself and a woman led her into the manager's office. She pushed her bangs from her eyes. She'd never get used to the new look. The man behind the desk stood and smiled at her.

"Miss Alton." He waved her to a chair. "I've been waiting for you to arrive. We are so glad you've chosen to settle in our little town. I'm sure you'll be happy here." He opened a drawer with a key from a heavy bunch and smiled at her. "Everything is ready to go." He slid a checkbook and ATM cards across the table. "It's just as you arranged."

She'd signed forms and the US Marshals had opened an account for her with a decent balance, but she'd made her own arrangements and there was no need for the marshals to know about her secret account. All she had to do was to pick up the ATM cards and set the PINs. She nodded and examined the cards. She pushed the card for her secret account toward him. "I'll need to transfer a substantial amount of money into this account at once and arrange payment for a ranch I've just purchased."

"Not a problem." The bank manager opened his hands wide. "I'm here to make all the necessary arrangements you need."

With ease, she transferred a considerable amount from her offshore account and arranged to have the new account trickle-fed by the interest. In the meantime, she had about six weeks before the house was settled to decide on furniture. But first, she'd make the arrangements to fix the problems on the inspection list. She bid farewell to the bank manager and hurried from the bank. After calling the contractors Susie Hartwig had suggested, she wanted to happy-dance. She owned a ranch!

Excited, she climbed into her vehicle and headed for the address Davis had given her. She found the small house on Main. It was a relief to be in the middle of town. With so many people walking by, it was doubtful anyone from her past would try anything. She bit her lip, thinking about living alone on the ranch. Would she ever stop looking over her shoulder? Stepping out of her vehicle, she stared at the rental. It was an older-style redbrick with a beautiful garden, neat and well-tended. She unloaded her bags from the vehicle and headed inside. The smell of beeswax and pine disinfectant greeted her. It was as neat as a pin. She walked around the house, peering into rooms and closets. Everything had been supplied. There were some canned goods, but she needed groceries. Being slap bang in the middle of town, she soon found all the stores she needed within walking distance. It was such a beautiful day she spent a couple of hours moving from store to store. Every place she went, the townsfolk greeted her like an old friend and there was genuine enthusiasm and offers of help when she told them she'd be making Black Rock Falls her home. They answered all her questions and she'd added to her list of recommended contractors. After some thought, she'd decided to divide the construction of the safe room into sections, giving each contractor a small piece of the puzzle. The reinforced door she'd purchase from another town and have the contractor deliver and install it. She'd use two security firms, one for the fence and another for the safe room and house. It would take a lot of planning, but it would be the only way to keep safe.

She spent a nice afternoon selecting and ordering furniture and household goods. Most of the suppliers had been able to fit in with her schedule. That night she climbed into bed relaxed and happy. *Now all I need is a job.*

THIRTEEN

The meeting with Mayor Rockford the following morning was interesting. Walters had already sworn Jenna in as a deputy. He'd given her a badge and a sheriff's department jacket, but she would have to wait for him to order her a uniform. The mayor agreed to allow her to campaign in the elections for the position of sheriff, but made it quite clear she'd have to prove herself as a deputy before she gained his vote. When Walters escorted her to enter her name on the ballot, she stared at him. "Are you sure the townsfolk will vote for me?"

"Of course, they will. You'll be just what the doctor ordered. A fresh broom as they say, and you won't have to worry. I've been deputy here for many years and people listen to me." Walters beamed at her. "We need new blood in town and, with your qualifications, you'll be the most suited for the job. I'll get you out meeting people and help you get everything printed up for your campaign." He gave a belly laugh. "We've been advertising for deputies for a time. Another one or maybe two will spread the workload. With the rodeo circuit and the festivals, not to mention the football and hockey, the more the merrier."

Slightly off kilter and overwhelmed by the speed things were happening, but determined to work her butt off to make the grade, Jenna slipped on the jacket, secured her badge, and smiled. "Okay. That's good to know. I guess we'd better head back to the sheriff's office. I'll need a duty belt if I'm going out on patrol."

As they arrived at the sheriff's office, she looked at Walters. "It's just as well you have men's uniforms on hand for any new deputies we can entice to join us. If I'm elected, I'll only be wearing the jacket. I move better in jeans and a T-shirt." She stopped at the sight of an attractive African American woman standing behind the front counter.

"Magnolia Brewster, meet our new deputy, hopefully to become our next sheriff, Jenna Alton." Walters grinned broadly. "Maggie here runs everything, answers the phone, and collects the fines."

Jenna smiled. "It's great to meet you, Maggie."

"Likewise, I'm sure." Maggie inclined her head. "Will you be wanting a duty belt? I have a few different sizes of the basic belt, but you're the smallest deputy we've had so far." She went to a chest of drawers and pulled out a belt. "Try this on for size."

Fitted out, with her own Glock in the holster, she smiled at Deputy Walters. "Okay, can I look through your case files? I'd like to be up to date."

As she headed to the office, a call came in about a disturbance at the local church. She followed Walters out to his cruiser and slipped inside. As they sped through town, she glanced at him. "What, did somebody take off with the poor box?"

"Not sure." He pulled up in front of the church. "Father Derry just said to get down here fast. I could hear shouting, so something's going down."

Jenna slid out the seat of the cruiser and headed for the church. A woman ran out screaming, her face bruised and blood dripping from a split lip. She held out an arm to slow the woman. "Hey, what's happening?"

"My ex-husband found me." She glanced over one shoulder and turned a panicked expression to Jenna. "He's set to kill me. I was hiding in the church." She waved a hand frantically toward the door. "Father Derry—"

"I'll speak to him when you're safe." Keeping her voice calm, Jenna led the woman to the cruiser and beckoned Walters over. "What's your name?"

"Carol, Carol Dean." The woman was shaking like a leaf.

Jenna took her by the arm. "You'll be safe with us. We'll deal with your ex. What's his name?"

"Errol... Errol Dean." Her eyes flashed with terror. "There he is now. Oh my God, he's coming." She cringed away.

The fact Jenna had never been a regular cop and had agents to back her up on busts all through her DEA career meant that facing a crazy man practically alone was going to be a new experience. Shooting him wasn't an option and in Black Rock Falls he could very well be loaded for bear. She had to prove she could do the job and pushed away the impending rush of inadequacy. This could be a make-or-break moment to prove herself. Taking a deep breath, she turned as a man in his thirties, wearing a T-shirt with a local football team's logo on the front, blue jeans, and a ballcap came hurtling toward them.

"He sure looks mad." Deputy Walters would be no match for a stronger younger man.

Jenna moved toward the running man and held up a hand in an effort to stop him. "Get her away from here. I'll deal with him. He's not carrying a weapon."

"Sure thing." Deputy Walters took hold of the woman's arm and led her away.

Fingers itching to pull her Glock, Jenna calmly drew her nightstick from her belt and shook it out to full length. At her time in rehab, she'd learned a few tricks, and kept her voice calm. "Okay, Errol. What's your story?"

"Get out of my way." Errol slid to a halt as mad as a bull and snorting through his nose. "I said get out of my way, lady."

After taking abuse from Michael and having to stand there and do nothing, she had firsthand knowledge of what his ex-wife had suffered. Yeah, she understood just fine that men like this didn't expect women to stand up to them. They enjoyed the power over a weaker person but most of them were cowards. "Sorry, I can't do that. Now how about you cool down some and we'll talk?"

The slap came so fast and hard Jenna's vision blurred. She tasted blood on her tongue but lifted her chin and glared at him. She'd never allow a man to hurt her again. "You might figure you can get away with a small fine or a day or so in jail for hitting your wife, but I'm a law enforcement officer." She took a breath watching him shape up to hit her again. "Bad mistake, Errol."

"I'm not afraid of you." He grinned. "I could break you in half like a twig."

Using her nightstick, Jenna swung it low and took out his legs. He howled like a wolf and cursed as he tumbled to the floor clutching at his shins. Dropping to her knees, she spun him onto his back and had him cuffed in seconds. Bending down close to his ear, she lowered her voice to a whisper. "That's how it feels when women fight back. I'm in town now. And I'll prosecute you to the full extent of the law." She helped him up and, taking a firm grip on the powerful man, she led him to the cruiser.

"If I can't have you, nobody can, Carol." Errol's face contorted into a mask of hate. "Think about that before I come see you again."

The taut muscles under Jenna's hand displayed a strength she wouldn't be able to control for long, and juiced up on adrenalin, this guy was dangerous. She had to get control and turned to Errol. "Get in the vehicle, you sack of shit." She sat him down, one hand on his head, and was about to close the door when it flew open. He barreled out, head down, and charged at her. "Hey."

The two-hundred-pound man clipped her with his shoulder as he ran past, tossing her to one side. Jenna rolled and grabbed Errol by the ankle, holding on tight, but he was intent on getting to the woman. Dragged along behind him, she watched in horror as Deputy Walters, his back turned, had missed the attempted escape. The next second, in a flash of denim, another man hit Errol with a shoulder charge and slammed him to the ground. The young man had his knee in Errol's back and had him pinned to the floor. He looked up at Jenna and blushed. "Ah... are you okay, Deputy?"

After dusting herself off, Jenna took charge of her prisoner. She read him his rights and this time, with the other man standing close by, Errol went into the back of the cruiser all the while screaming "police brutality." She closed the door and turned to the tall man with curly brown hair. "Thank you. He's a slippery one. I'm glad you came along. You're very fast. Are you in law enforcement?"

"Not yet." He picked up his Stetson, dusted it on his leg, and then held out his hand. "Jake Rowley. I'm back home from college and was looking to join the sheriff's department." He turned to Deputy Walters. "I was coming by to speak to you and saw you parked here. I wanted to discuss the position of deputy you advertised." He glanced at Jenna. "Seems I'm too late."

Jenna looked him over. She needed a strong deputy as a partner. Walters was obviously having trouble getting around and didn't hear too well. "Maybe not. Can you hang around for a time? I need to call the paramedics for Mrs. Dean."

"You'll need to go check on Father Derry." Mrs. Dean pointed to the church. "Errol knocked him down."

"I'll call the paramedics." Jake Rowley pulled out his phone. "And I'll be happy to wait here with Mrs. Dean."

"My name is Carol." She patted her cut lip with a tissue and looked at Jenna. "Thanks for your help." She moved her gaze to Rowley. "I hope you make it as a deputy. We need some muscle around town."

"I'll wait here with the prisoner, Jenna. Go see Father Derry." Walters leaned against the cruiser. "Give me a yell if you need any help."

FOURTEEN

Finding it hard to believe Walters had thrust her into a situation without a second thought—or backup—Jenna bit back a snort of incredulity and hurried for the church. Poor old Deputy Walters was breathing so hard she couldn't imagine how he'd coped since the sheriff died. She stepped inside the large carved wooden doors and the smell of burning candles hit her in a wave of memories. Her parents' funeral still lingered in the dark recesses of her mind, and the fresh wound of losing Steve came back in a rush. Coming from bright sunlight into the muted light inside the church, she blinked a few times as her eyes adjusted and she scanned the interior. "Father Derry?"

A moan came from one end of the pews. She walked past the confessional boxes and she found a middle-aged man crumpled on the floor. Blood trickled from a cut on his head and dripped from his chin to a crimson patch on his pristine white collar. She dropped to her knees and examined him closely. "Father Derry. Open your eyes."

"Who are you?" Father Derry blinked a few times and then pushed into a sitting position, with his back against the wall. "Where's Carol?"

"I'm Deputy Jenna Alton and Carol is outside waiting for the paramedics with Deputy Walters." She pulled a pack of tissues from her pocket and handed him a few. "What happened here?"

"Carol is one of my parishioners. She came here for sanctuary. I provide a safe place for people in need." He waved to his face. "Unfortunately, her husband arrived before I was able to get her to safety. I was knocked over and hit my head."

Jenna frowned. "Carol mentioned they'd recently divorced."

"Not in the eyes of the church." Father Derry sighed. "Although I did offer them counselling, I can't unfortunately work miracles."

"So it would seem." Jenna heard a siren in the distance. "Stay where you are. I'll go and meet the paramedics." She patted his shoulder and stood.

Outside, an ambulance pulled up and two paramedics jumped out. She waved one toward the church. "Father Derry has a head injury and facial bruising. He was unconscious when I found him, but he seems lucid now."

"Okay, lead the way." The paramedic followed her inside, carrying his bag.

After examining the priest, the paramedic insisted he went to the ER. Jenna waited with Father Derry while the paramedic went to fetch a gurney and then loaded up the priest. She squeezed the poor man's arm. "Is there anyone I can call?"

"Would you go and tell my housekeeper what's happened? In the rectory round back." Father Derry gripped her arm. "She'll know what to do."

Jenna nodded. "Don't worry, I'll go and see her as soon as I've checked on Carol."

On her return to the cruiser, Deputy Walters surprised her by waving a statement book in front of her face. She shook her head. "Not yet. Father Derry has a head injury. I'll speak to him later about making a statement."

"Not the good father. Carol Dean has given a statement. She doesn't want Errol getting away with hurting Father Derry or her this time." Walters indicated to the ambulance. "She's going to the ER as well. I figure they'll both be kept there overnight for tests and observation. I've contacted Carol's folks and they'll meet her there."

"Okay." Jenna glanced behind her. "Where's the rectory?"

"Rowley here will show you." Walters smiled at her. "He's a local boy. I figure we need a rookie for someone of your experience to supervise. What do you say, Jenna? I can swear him in today and he can start tomorrow."

"I'm standing right here." Jake Rowley looked from one to the other. "Maybe you two should discuss it some?"

Jenna cleared her throat. He had a point, and she didn't like him putting her on the spot in front of a potential rookie candidate. "Good idea." She raised her eyebrows at Walters and walked some distance away. "First up, is there room in the budget for another deputy?"

"Another two, and if you become sheriff, I'll go into semi-retirement. I'll just come in when you need me." Walters rested his hand on his weapon. "The town isn't poor by any means, Jenna. It's prosperous and the town council runs all the festivals and tourist events. They make a good deal of money and it's only going to get better. The mayor and local business owners are making plans to increase the tourist attractions. I hear tell of plans for a ski resort and a whitewater-rapid attraction, plus tour guides for those people who want to hike. And of course, we have those people who come here to hunt and fish."

Trying to take it all in at once, Jenna nodded slowly. "Ah... getting back to Jake Rowley. I assume you ran a background check on me before you offered me a badge. How come you're offering to deputize this guy, who just walked up to you on the street?"

"Jake Rowley?" Walters laughed. "I've known him since he was knee-high to a grasshopper. He's smart and holds a black belt in martial arts, took out the last competition on rifle marksmanship, and played college football. Townsfolk like him and he's wanted to be in law enforcement since he could speak."

Jenna stared at her boots, and then lifted her gaze to look at the old man. "So why isn't he going for sheriff?"

"He has no experience, but he learns real fast. But he has one tiny chink in his armor." Walters chuckled. "He's not so good when it comes to the sight of blood—as in a messy crime scene, but as we don't have mass murder in Black Rock Falls, he should fit in just fine." He opened his hands. "You know, after seeing how you handled Dean, I'll be speaking to Mayor Rockford. I figure you should take over from me as acting sheriff. With Rowley to back you up, you'll handle things just fine. I'm happy to be a desk jockey. My days of handling men like Errol Dean are over."

"Okay. That's fine by me." Jenna nodded. Her first few hours on the job and she'd taken over already. "With Jake to show me around, I'll be just fine." She walked back toward Rowley.

"Good, I'll go speak to the mayor when we get back to the office." Walters grinned at Rowley. "Welcome to the team. If the mayor agrees, and I can be darn right persuasive, Jenna here will take over as acting sheriff until the elections. I'll expect you to show her around, and let the townsfolk know we have an experienced law enforcement officer on our team."

"Thanks, I'll get the word out." Rowley turned to Jenna. "I know me just showing up here looks kind of suspicious." He gave her a lopsided smile. "My folks just live down the road a ways." He pointed to a pathway heading round the back of the church. "The rectory is through there."

Jenna liked his honest face and walked beside him. "What was your major at college?"

"Social sciences." Rowley followed her along the pathway. "Do you mind me asking what you did before you arrived here?"

Jenna glanced over her shoulder at him. "Not at all. I was a detective. I left because of some personal problems. I wanted a fresh start and figured Black Rock Falls looked like an ideal place to live." She smiled at him. "I arrived in town yesterday and purchased a ranch. This morning I became a deputy and made my first arrest."

"Holy cow!" Rowley laughed. "And now you've had a promotion." He glanced at his watch. "It's not even noon yet. You sure don't let the grass grow under your feet, ma'am."

After speaking with Father Derry's housekeeper and mentioning Carol Dean, she discovered the priest was very proactive when it came to caring for his parishioners. He ran a soup kitchen and used a building in town to give temporary accommodation to anyone in trouble. A place would be available to Carol Dean when she came out of the hospital. The volunteers who ran everything came mainly from his congregation, and he rarely turned anyone away from Our Lady's Sanctuary, but it had its limits. The overflow had to be housed elsewhere but the homeless didn't get the same automatic pass into the municipal shelters. It had only been in the last year, after the long winter had caused great hardship that the town council decided to convert the abandoned sawmill into two facilities: New Start for men and New Hope for women.

She headed back to the cruiser with Rowley by her side and glanced up at him. "Can you start today? I don't figure Walters is well enough to be showing me around."

"Sure." He headed for his truck. "I'll meet you at the office."

She gave him a wave and headed back to the cruiser. As she

climbed inside, she looked at Walters. "How many vehicles do we have?"

"Two cruisers and a truck." Walters eased his bulk behind the wheel. "I figure the cruisers are useless for Black Rock Falls. The truck is a little more up to date. Maybe now you're here, you'll be able to loosen the town council's purse strings. We need updated vehicles. The truck belonged to the sheriff. It's the newest vehicle we have and the only one that would make it safely up the mountain."

Jenna nodded. "Have they been maintained regularly?"

"Sure, at George's Garage here in town." Walters smiled. "But you can't make a silk purse out of a sow's ear." He started the engine and they headed back into town.

"Hey. You know darn well Carol won't press charges. Might as well let me out now." Errol Dean's voice came from behind them, slightly muffled by the acrylic screen.

"Not this time." Walters glanced in his rearview mirror.

"Aw, come on. You won't stand up for this stupid woman." Dean's voice sounded confident. "She provoked me, and you darn well know it."

"That's not what I saw, and we have another witness." Walters cleared his throat. "Deputy Alton will press charges."

"So, I'm sorry, okay?" Dean leaned forward and pressed his nose on the acrylic divider. "Where are you taking me?"

Jenna turned in her seat to stare at him. "To jail. Where you belong."

FIFTEEN

Temper rising, Errol Dean clenched his fists so tight his knuckles ached. He stared at his lawyer, James Stone. "First up, I didn't hit Carol. I came down to the church to talk to her is all. That deputy, the smart-mouthed woman, got between me and my wife. She was arresting her and I was trying to save her."

"The deputy's made a complaint against you for striking her." Stone looked up from his paperwork. "I'd say Deputy Walters will bear witness and then there's Father Derry."

Snorting, Dean shook his head. "Well, Deputy Walters was facing the other way and talking to Carol at the time, so I'd say he's telling lies. What happened is I got to the church and there was Carol all banged up. I went toward her to comfort her, and she ran away screaming, knocking over Father Derry, and running out the door. The priest was out cold and I went after Carol. I wanted to find out who had hit her, for as sure as hell it wasn't me. What did I see? The new deputy, pushing her toward a cruiser." He stared at James Stone. "What would you do?"

"I'd ask why she was being arrested, but apparently that isn't the case here." Stone held up a statement. "Deputy Alton states she sent Carol around the other side of the cruiser with Deputy Walters to protect her from you."

Unable to believe what he was saying, Dean shook his head. "She hadn't even seen me at the time. Like I said, when I came out the church, Deputy Alton was leading Carol to the cruiser. They need to get their facts straight. She had her back turned. It would have been impossible to have seen me."

"Okay, but Father Derry made a complaint saying there was a problem at the church." Stone cleared his throat. "You saying you didn't hit the priest?"

Dean met his gaze. "I didn't hit the priest." He thought for a beat. "This is confidential isn't it—between you and me? You ain't going to rat me out to the cops?"

"No, we have attorney-client privilege. Nothing you say to me leaves this room." Stone leaned forward resting his hands on the table. "I can only defend you if you tell me the truth. Lies come undone under cross-examination, and we don't want that now, do we?"

Rubbing the back of his neck, Dean nodded. "I have hit Carol in the past but not today. That's why she divorced me, but it isn't final yet and I want her back."

"So, you're saying, you didn't hit Deputy Alton, Carol, or Father Derry?" Stone picked up his pen and made notes on a legal pad.

"Nope or that woman. Deputy Alton was arresting me without reading me my rights. She didn't as much as tell me I was being arrested. She just hit me with her nightstick and cuffed me." Dean spread his hands on the table. "Look here, if I'd punched Carol in the mouth, my knuckles would be damaged, same with the priest. I don't have a mark on me. I do admit to knocking the deputy over. She got in my way when I was getting out the back of the cruiser. She's a little thing and I clipped her with my shoulder is all."

"Okay. Now a recap. Are you one hundred percent sure

Deputy Walters and Carol had their backs turned when Deputy Alton hit you with her nightstick?" Stone held the pen just above the paper and raised both eyebrows.

Getting at the angle his lawyer was taking, Dean smiled on the inside. He liked this guy's style. "No, they didn't witness her police brutality and, like I said, during the time she said I hit her, they had their backs turned."

"And Father Derry won't testify that you hit him?" Stone made copious notes.

Dean had already considered this possibility. He'd confess his sins and ask for forgiveness from the good father. There'd be no way he'd bear witness against him in court. "Nope."

"It seems to me all they can actually charge you with is resisting arrest and assault on a police officer. You could get five years for assaulting a police officer in the performance of their duties." Stone leaned back in his chair. "They've defined the assault—in the statement it doesn't mention that you knocked her over. It says an openhanded slap and you dispute that, but if knocking her down is under their definition of resisting arrest and you plead guilty, you may walk or get a month, maybe two." He sighed. "The magistrate's list is open. You'll get bail this afternoon, if we can push this through now. Plead guilty and, worse case, you do a month in county."

Thinking, Dean stared at his hands. "And if the DA believes the cops? I get five years, right?"

"That's why you pay me the big bucks." James Stone smiled at him. "We'll do an interview, but allow me to do most of the talking. I'll shoot their charges down in flames."

SIXTEEN

The morning had turned into a whirlwind of a day for Jenna. After locking up Errol Dean and contacting the only available lawyer in town, James Stone, to represent him, she went over her list of charges and waited to interview her prisoner. To Jenna's surprise, Mayor Rockford walked into the office and went straight to her desk. "Can I help you, Mayor Rockford?"

"You sure can." He gave her a skeptical look. Walters had obviously called him about finding a replacement. "Stand up, Deputy Alton. It seems I have little choice but to swear you in as Black Rock Falls acting sheriff—it's only temporary. We'll see who the townsfolk decide on at the election."

Being sworn in was surreal. Convinced she'd wake up soon and find herself still on the flight to Black Rock Falls, Jenna took the badge he offered her and stared at it in disbelief. "Thank you. I won't let you down."

"You can be assured I'll be watching you very closely." Mayor Rockford frowned. "Maybe the townsfolk will come to you to complain instead of me for a change."

At least, I'll do something. Jenna lifted her chin and took in the measure of the man. There was something about him she didn't like. She had that gnawing in her gut that told her something about his overzealous charm wasn't quite right. Pushing down her rising doubt, she nodded. "I'll be sure to listen and deal with any problems that arise. I don't particularly like the lenient spousal abuse laws you have, and I'll be using whatever powers I have at my disposal to make sure women and any men who are being abused are protected."

"Well, the majority decides in this town. If you want my advice, leave it until after the election. You don't want to turn the folks against you. People in Black Rock Falls don't like change." Rockford gave her a nod of dismissal and glided out the office on a cloud of cologne.

Trying to keep her mind on the task at hand, Jenna swore in Jake Rowley and had Walters organize his uniforms and weapon. She walked out to speak to Maggie on the front counter. "Where is the sheriff's office? Is there a room set aside here or do we all work at these desks?"

"The sheriff's office is that door over there." Maggie's eyes dropped to the counter. "No one has been in there since the sheriff died. His wife came and took his nameplate from the door, seeing she'd paid for it herself." She lifted her gaze. "I have the keys right here." She opened a drawer, took out a bunch of keys and handed them to her.

"Okay, thanks." Jenna smiled. "Can you order a nameplate that just says SHERIFF for me, please?"

"Right away." Maggie smiled and her eyes lit up. "It's sure good having you in town, Jenna."

Smiling, Jenna headed for the door. "I'll get at it. Give me a call when Mr. Stone allows me to interview the prisoner."

The office smelled of stale air heavy with the odor of musky male sweat. Not the kind from a freshly showered hardworking male, but sour like an unwashed sock. She pinched her nose and flung open the windows. A cool breeze rushed inside, bringing with it the scent of pine trees with a hint of freshly baked bread.

She stood for a moment, taking in the panoramic vista before her. The sheriff's department sat on the highest point of Main, to the south she could see all the way down Main to the park and even make out the sign over Aunt Betty's Café. To the north, Main turned into Stanton and bordered Stanton Forest, a boundless sea of pine trees that ended at the foot of a mountain range of black granite bearing the name of the town and county. Blue skies stretched out without a cloud in sight and in the distance two eagles soared, gliding around in circles on a thermal current. It was as if she'd stepped into a dream, for nothing before this had ever looked so beautiful.

With reluctance, she turned back to the messy office. It could be nice again with a good cleaning. The room held a whiteboard, a good wide desk, chairs, and a computer that could probably do with an update. Filing cabinets stood to one side and under the window was a small kitchenette. A refrigerator under a benchtop, a sink, a coffeemaker with a line of green mold floating on top, and a pile of dirty cups and plates. Along one wall was a closet and a gun locker displaying a good selection of weapons: pistols, rifles, and shotguns.

She checked out the mess on the table and found nothing of interest. Newspapers and scribbled notes she tossed into the trash. She found a daybook inside the desk drawer and flipped through it finding nothing of great interest at all. Missing dogs, traffic violations, and reports of sales of stolen Native American artifacts at the last rodeo, but it seemed the previous sheriff had done nothing to apprehend the culprits.

She heard a sound at the door and turned to see Maggie. "Has Mr. Stone finished?"

"Yeah, he said you can speak to his client now." Maggie peered around the room. "It's a bit of a mess. The old sheriff didn't like the cleaners coming in. He preferred it lived in, so he said."

Jenna wrinkled her nose. "What's the chance of getting a

crew in to clean this place up? I can't work in here and I won't have time to fix it up myself." She glanced back at the room. "I don't have a problem paying for it myself, if necessary."

"You won't have to do that. I'll send the bill to the town council as usual." Maggie smiled. "I'll get at it now." She headed back to her desk.

After discovering Rowley was well versed in Montana law, she pulled up her files on police procedure and sat him down before her laptop. "While we have some downtime, familiarize yourself with the procedure for various crime scenes and situations. Learn how to Mirandize a suspect, take statements, process a crime scene, and collect evidence. You'll need to know when to arrest someone and when to take them in for questioning."

"I'm a fast learner and I know most of this stuff. I've always wanted to be a deputy." He glanced at the screen. "Can I copy the files onto a thumb drive to study at home?"

Welcoming his enthusiasm, she smiled. "Sure. You'll learn along the way too, riding out with me every day. As soon as I'm settled, we'll take in the practice range and find a place where I can train you. Taking down a suspect is a little different than martial arts, although you handled yourself real good today."

"We can use my dojo. There are times when the hall is free, and I only have to ask." Rowley grinned. "I help out there by teaching some of the kids, so I get perks."

Jenna laughed. "Sounds good to me." She snatched up a statement book from the desk and headed for the cells, stopping at Deputy Walters' desk. "It's time to interview Errol Dean. I'm going to make darn sure he can't worm his way out of the charges."

SEVENTEEN

The interview room had the distinct odor of a football locker room and Jenna made a mental note to purchase plug-in air fresheners for every room in the building. Wrinkling her nose, she stepped inside with Deputy Walters close behind. As she placed her file on the table and slid out a notepad, Walters turned on the video recording device using a remote and Jenna could see the screen frozen on pause. She took her seat across the desk from her prisoner and his lawyer and looked at James Stone. "Are you ready to proceed?"

"We are." Stone's mouth twitched up at the corners in a satisfied smirk.

Jenna indicated to Walters to start the recordings. She gave the time and date and asked all present to identify themselves. "Mr. Dean was Mirandized at the scene." She gave details of the charges. "Mr. Dean, from Carol Dean's statement, she divorced you after constant spousal abuse and claims you continue to strike her."

"Do you have proof that Mrs. Dean is telling the truth?" James Stone's dark gaze rested on her. "Any witness statements, hospital records?"

Jenna stared right back at him. "You should be aware that we are in the discovery stage of the investigation at the moment. This interview is to determine if we keep Mr. Dean here for further questioning or make formal charges." She lifted her chin. "However, he struck an officer in the performance of their duty and resisted arrest."

"Hmm." Stone shook his head slowly. "I'm not seeing any statements to back up that accusation." He turned to Deputy Walters. "Did you actually see my client, strike Deputy... ah... Acting Sheriff Alton?"

"No, by the time I turned around, everyone was on the ground." Walters scratched his head. "So, in fact, I only witnessed Mr. Dean resisting arrest."

By this time, Errol Dean was grinning like a cat who'd got the cream. Jenna's stomach dropped, but she moved on. "Then there's the attack on Father Derry and I can bear witness that you were chasing after Carol, who I could plainly see had taken a beating."

"I didn't touch Father Derry or Carol." Dean leaned forward on the table so close she could smell his cigarette-tainted breath. "Yeah, I was chasing after her—to see if she was okay. You went way off base hitting me with your nightstick, and that guy who tackled me bruised my ribs."

Jenna shrugged. "We had a call about a disturbance at the church. You posed a threat and I was well within my rights to detain you for questioning."

"Seems to me"—James Stone opened his hands wide—"all you have is resisting arrest and maybe a very slight chance of the court believing my client hit Carol. The rest is hearsay and, I might add, as the striking charge came from you, Acting Sheriff, you just being in this room is a conflict of interest. Are you carrying out some sort of illegal vendetta against my client?"

She kicked herself as she realized that Stone was correct. In hindsight she should have asked Walters to interview the prisoner, but being so short-staffed, what option did she have? She nodded slowly. "Very well, I'll withdraw the striking charge, but the resisting arrest remains, as does the assault on Carol Dean."

"Minor offenses will be dealt with by the magistrate, but I figure he'll think you're just wasting his time." Stone pushed his legal pad into a briefcase and dropped it beside him. "Write it up, see the DA, or whatever you feel you need to do, but I want my client before the magistrate for a bail hearing this afternoon."

It was as if he'd dismissed her. She looked at Dean. "I'll be recommending Carol take out a protective order against you. You may walk this time, but it won't happen again."

"Are you threatening me, Sheriff?" Dean smiled at her. "On tape and in front of my lawyer too. Nice try."

Jenna pushed to her feet. "That wasn't a threat, Mr. Dean. It was a statement of truth. I'm planning on standing up for the victims of spousal abuse by making darn sure they're protected by law." She picked up the remote and turned off the recorder. "Deputy Walters, will you escort the prisoner back to the cells?" As Walters left leading Dean away, she turned to James Stone. "There's coffee in the main office, if you'd like to wait while I write up the paperwork."

"Thanks, I don't have too much to do right now." Stone rested one hip on the corner of the table and his expression softened. "Tough first day, huh?"

Surprised by his sudden turnaround from hardnosed lawyer to normal guy, Jenna laughed. "I've had worse." She leaned against the wall. "You came on pretty strong. I figured we were enemies. It's nice to see a different side to you."

"When it comes down to convicting an innocent man, I'm one uncompromising SOB, but I handle deceased estates, wills... well, just about everything, so I do have a heart." Stone opened his hands wide. "Although, there's no police prosecutor in town for me to spar with. The DA handles all the prosecutions." He frowned and looked at his hands. "He is one of the smartest attorneys I've met. He doesn't mince words and gives it to you straight. In court, he makes my life hell."

Jenna walked out into the passageway with Stone close behind. "Well, I guess I'm going to find out myself in a few minutes." She looked at him over one shoulder. "If you can point me in the direction of his office?"

"Two down from Aunt Betty's Café. The tall redbrick. His office is on the second floor." Stone headed for the coffee pot. "Good luck!"

* * *

Being used to the slow drag of red tape and bureaucracy in the city, Jenna hadn't expected things to move so fast. Black Rock Falls had little crime and, with only neighborhood disputes and traffic offences to deal with, the court lists remained virtually empty. The DA took the same stance as James Stone and waved away the unsubstantiated attack on her, but he would proceed with the assault on Carol Dean and the charge of resisting arrest. He agreed to filing the protection order and arranged for both matters to be dealt with that afternoon.

In most cases, lawyers needed months, sometimes years, to prepare for a case, but it seemed in this town the legal process moved at warp speed. When James Stone addressed the court and instructed the judge that his client had decided to plead guilty to expedite matters, the magistrate laid down the sentencing phase for three days hence. The speedy court date astounded her. More so when the magistrate gave Errol Dean bail with his ex-wife still in the hospital and vulnerable.

As she walked back to the office, her neck prickled and she turned to see Errol Dean leaning against the wall of the general store staring at her. She'd walked right by him and been so involved with her thoughts on the speedy judicial system that she hadn't noticed him. When he gave her a smile and tipped his hat, she caught the sadistic expression in his eyes. He reminded her of Michael and the smug way he'd look at her after he'd hit her. A too familiar trapped feeling enclosed her in a rush of memories and she fought back the terrible need to run and keep going. Seeing the welcoming sign outside Aunt Betty's Café, she pushed through the door. The bell tinkled and a warm delicious smell engulfed her. People looked up from their meals and smiled. A wall of safety enclosed her and she could suddenly breathe again. Her stomach growled and she remembered in all the excitement she hadn't eaten since leaving home. She ordered from the counter and made her way to the table reserved for the sheriff's department and sat down. Gathering her thoughts, she called Maggie to inform her when she'd be back at the office. She scanned the menu to pass the time and started when she glanced up to see James Stone walking to her table. *What the hell do you want?*

EIGHTEEN

The last thing Jenna needed was the attention of James Stone. Although, Stone was quite handsome and he'd be a good catch if she wanted a husband, but she wasn't interested. Losing Steve in such a brutal fashion still hurt. She'd loved him, his funny smile, and sense of humor. He'd had her back and had died protecting her. If things had worked out differently, they'd have made a good couple. The wash of Stone's cologne tainted the delicious aromas of the café but she composed her face and looked at him. "Is there something I can do for you, Mr. Stone?"

"Maybe ask me to join you for a start, people are looking at us." He raised one dark eyebrow and his hand went to the back of the chair.

Smothering a much-needed eyeroll, Jenna nodded. "Sure, take a seat. What's on your mind?"

"I noticed Errol Dean giving you the stink eye before, and I figured if I came by and sat at your table, he'd get the message and go home." He waved to Susie and ordered a pulled-pork roll with fries. "I didn't dispute the fact he hit his wife and, off the record, did he really strike you or were you just trying to get him off the streets?"

Running her tongue over the inside of her split lip, Jenna eyeballed him. "One thing we need to get straight from the get-go: I never and will never fabricate charges against anyone." She pulled down her lip to display the injury and then scowled at him, but kept her voice low so only he could hear. "Yeah, he slapped me, but I don't go down easy. Cowards like him don't know how to cope with a woman who stands up to them." She leaned forward and caught the change in his eyes. It was almost a challenge. "If I make sheriff, I'm going to stand up for anyone in town suffering abuse, men, women, or kids. From what I see, this is a culture that needs to change. Bullies don't rule the world and when a person marries, they no longer become someone's property. Those days are long gone."

"Ouch." Stone leaned back in his seat and smiled. "The lady has been hurt." He sipped his coffee and peered at her for a beat. "I like a woman who fights back. It makes life so much more interesting."

NINETEEN

TWO MONTHS LATER

Life ran as smooth as silk in Black Rock Falls. Jenna had slipped into her job without a problem. She'd held the first rally in the town hall for her election campaign for sheriff and the towns-folk loved her. The fact Mayor Rockford had introduced her as a highly trained detective had made a good impression and, with some time yet to prove her worth, she considered herself a good chance to win. Many people appreciated the way she'd pursued a conviction against Errol Dean. Although he'd been locked away in county jail and had completed a one-month sentence, the protection order for his wife was still in place and Jenna had arranged an apartment for Carol above the hardware store in town. The location was perfect and not only close to the sheriff's department. But Deputy Walters lived on Maple, the road running parallel to Main, so if Dean caused a problem, Carol had law enforcement close by.

The community spirit in town impressed Jenna. It was so different to the indifference she'd witnessed in some big cities. If someone was down on their luck in Black Rock Falls, their neighbors would help out. During a recent storm, lightning caused a fire in a cattle rancher's barn, and destroyed not only the building but also his winter feed stocks. As soon as the townsfolk discovered the poor man was in trouble, posters for a barn-raising appeared all over town. The people had gotten together, fixed his barn, and donated feed. Rowley had informed her this wasn't unusual for the townsfolk and promised she'd get to see the community enthusiasm during the festivals that came thick and fast all year long.

Impressed by Jake Rowley's eagerness, she'd spent hours working with him. She'd soon discovered her day's work often included going deep into Stanton Forest, and only a few of the trails were negotiable by her vehicle. She'd never owned or cared for a horse and her only experience on horseback had been on a pony at a kid's birthday party. In Black Rock Falls, knowing how to ride and ride well was essential. When she informed Rowley, she'd expected him to ridicule her, but on the contrary, he'd offered to teach her. They'd spent hours at his parents' ranch, with her riding his mother's gentle sorrel mare before venturing into the forest. She appreciated Rowley's knowledge of the county, and when he'd insisted on taking her over a variety of terrains to make her proficient, she'd jumped at the chance.

He was just about the nicest young man she'd met in a long time and had the quiet disposition and even temper she appreciated. Although, he called her "ma'am," which made her feel like his grandma, but that was just being polite around these parts. The longer she mingled with the townsfolk, the more she understood their ways. After living in big cities all her life, the old-school ways were both refreshing and at the same time annoying. When she discussed alterations to the ranch house, for instance, she found some of the older folk went to great pains to explain things to her as if she'd just left kindergarten.

According to James Stone, the transfer of the house deeds would be through within the week. Jenna needed to clean the house so it was ready for the furniture to arrive and be there to open up for the contractors to start work. Once the house was secure, she'd move right in and supervise the alterations. She'd packed her things and stowed them in her cruiser, only keeping a few changes of clothes at the house. The moment she had the green light, she'd be moving out of the stuffy little rental and had already contacted the power company and purchased everything she needed to clean the ranch house. After dropping by to see Mr. Davis at the real estate office and explaining she needed to take measurements, he'd handed over the keys to the ranch.

Excited to be visiting her new home again, she made her way through town and out onto the highway. She had a wonderful feeling of freedom as she opened the gate and drove up the driveway. Being alone without Mr. Davis's voice echoing around the empty house, she actually really looked at the property. It was better than she remembered. The previous owners had lovingly renovated the house and kept the old-world charm but added a modern kitchen and bathrooms. In the family room a large marble fireplace dominated a huge room and underfoot they'd polished the wooden floors to such a high shine they looked as if they'd coated them in honey. All the bedrooms had their own bathrooms with separate showers. It seemed they'd spared no expense. She couldn't imagine working so hard on a house just to walk away, leaving all the memories of a growing family behind. As she cleaned the mantel, she could almost see the rows of framed photographs of the family. Maybe when their kids left for California, not being close had been too hard to bear. She had no photographs to place on the mantel, not that she would dare to add images of her parents for fear of the cartel finding her. One person recognizing them would discover she'd changed her identity. It wasn't worth the risk, and when she'd left her life behind, she'd taken nothing from her past life, not even a single pair of earrings.

She pushed away all thoughts of her parents and looked

ahead. She loved the town and her house, and she'd never imagined in her wildest dreams owning a ranch. It was surreal and she aimed to make it her sanctuary. After taking all the measurements she needed and making headway on cleaning half the house, she went outside to sit on the porch steps to take in the view. Weekends to herself were a luxury. She'd rarely had downtime in the DEA but here in this sleepy little town, she'd found time to go to the practice ranges with Rowley and just stroll around Main. Although over the last day or so, she'd had the nagging feeling someone was watching her. The fact that Errol Dean had been released from jail might have had her on alert, but he'd kept a low profile and she hadn't seen him. Just to be certain he was obeying the protection order, she'd asked Walters and Rowley to drop by from time to time and make sure Carol was okay. Carol had gotten a job at the Reef and Beef in town and seemed to be coping well.

As she took in the view, a glint in the hillside caught her attention. While inspecting the property, she'd explored the hill on the border, noting the other side had a pastoral trail that led to the highway. In fact, the woodlands over the boundary had tracks leading to most of the other properties, and she assumed, back when the Mitcham family owned most of the land on this side of the highway, they'd used the trails to move cattle from one grazing area to the next. The glint came again and she focused on the area. She shifted to one side and the glint came again. Self-preservation slammed into her and, heart pounding, she dived into the house slamming the door behind her. As her ranch house was the last building on the road apart from a couple of old barns on the corner, no one should be on the Mitcham's cursed land. Her stomach cramped. There could be only two explanations: She'd caught the glint from a rifle scope or someone was watching her through binoculars. Had Viktor found her?

Think, Jenna. She crawled into the mudroom and pressed

her back against the wall. The cold from the stone slabs under her seeped through her clothes, but beads of sweat trickled down her back. *How could they possibly know I'm here?*

Not expecting any trouble, she'd come unarmed and stored her Glock in the glovebox of her vehicle outside. She'd left the sheriff department's vehicle in the lot behind the office as it needed a serious update. It would be the first request she'd give the mayor if she made sheriff, but in the meantime her rental would have to do. Taking a few deep breaths, and keeping low, she headed for the kitchen. If someone was out in the hills with a rifle, then she'd lock up and, using the trees around the house for cover, would head for her truck. The woods along the driveway would give her protection to get onto the highway. Keeping her back to the wall, she edged into the kitchen and called Rowley. "Hey, it's Jenna. Sorry to bother you on the weekend, but I'm out at my ranch and caught sight of a reflection in the hill opposite, maybe binoculars or a scope. It may be nothing, but I'm calling in case it escalates into something. There shouldn't be anyone up there."

"You sure it's not the sun hitting a piece of glass or some foil maybe a bird dropped?" Rowley cleared his throat. *"Like you say, no one goes on the Old Mitcham Ranch and everyone figures that land is cursed. You'd heard tell about the curse when you purchased the property, right, ma'am?"*

Jenna pushed hair from her eyes and sighed. "Yeah, but curses don't reflect sunlight."

"That's for sure, but if a bird was carrying foil in its beak, it might catch the sun." Rowley sounded skeptical. *"I've seen crows do that many a time."*

Thinking it through, Jenna shook her head. "Nope, not crows. It moved when I moved. It followed me. Someone is watching me."

"Why would they do that?" Rowley's voice lowered and Jenna could hear voices close by. *"Who would know or care*

about you moving into the O'Reilly Ranch? Could it relate to the personal problem you left behind?"

Jenna eased out the back door and locked it, pushing the keys into her pocket. Having Rowley on the phone was better than being alone. "I'm not sure. I didn't tell anyone I planned to come here." She sighed. "Maybe I'm overreacting. I'm heading back to town as soon as I can get to my truck."

"I'll drive out and meet you on the highway. I'm just leaving the dojo." She could hear Rowley's boots on tile and then the sounds of traffic. *"If someone is following you, for whatever reason, they won't be expecting me to show."*

"Thanks, I'd appreciate it." Jenna disconnected. She sneaked through the long grass behind the house and slipped into the trees, suddenly glad about the overgrown state of her yard.

From the trees she had a good view of the hillside and scanned the area, breaking it into grids. Nothing glinted in the sunshine. *You're acting like a scared rabbit. For goodness sake, get a grip, woman.*

She headed back to her truck, slipped behind the wheel, and took a long look at her new home. She'd wanted isolation and privacy, but she'd only been here one morning and something had spooked her. It was her dream home but would it become a nightmare?

TWENTY

Jenna took off at top speed, spinning her wheels as she backed around, sending a cloud of dust high into the air. She pointed the truck at the driveway and fishtailed onto the blacktop. The rental truck was a basic model and didn't pull away as fast as she'd hoped, but it would be hard to shoot anyone moving at high speed. The grassy lowlands flew by in a sandy-colored tangle of dried grasses and bushes. Across the blacktop the shadows from the woodlands flickered like a silent movie. She glanced in the rearview mirror, but no one had followed her. She took the first long curve, blocking the view behind her, and kept up her speed until she went past the old barn and turned onto the highway. As she headed toward town, she had a sudden pang of regret and slowed down. She'd acted like a scared rabbit and run away, leaving her property open to anyone who ventured past. Maybe she should stop worrying about nothing and turn back and padlock the gate?

The next second, a white pickup came past her like she'd been standing still and cut right in front of her. Red taillights flashed as they made to stop. Jenna hit the brakes and the truck tires screamed in protest. The smell of burning rubber filled the cab as the back bounced and slid to one side. Spinning the wheel to gain control proved useless as the truck slid across the blacktop. In a bone-jarring jolt the front wheels dropped into the ditch alongside the road, throwing her forward with force. Airbags blocked her vision and the engine sighed and stalled. Batting the airbags away, she pressed the starter button and the engine shook and rattled but refused to start.

Looking all around but seeing no other vehicles on the road, she used the key to open the glovebox and pulled out her Glock. If that vehicle came back, she'd be ready. Not taking her eyes off the highway, she tried to recall details of the truck. It was a white pickup, no signage, and with the plate disguised with mud, it could be any one of the hundred or so she'd seen driven by locals, including herself. It seemed there must have been a special on white trucks in this town. She tried to start the engine a few more times without success and decided to keep watching the highway, hoping Rowley wouldn't be too long. The first vehicle to come by was an old blue pickup. It slowed and then backed up and an old white-haired man opened his window to stare at her.

"Do you need any help, ma'am?"

Jenna smiled. "No, I'm good. Thanks for stopping." She noticed Rowley's truck hurtling toward her at full speed and waved a hand toward him. "That's my help now. I'll be fine."

The old man drove on and a minute later Rowley pulled to the side of the highway and slid out of his truck. "Some jerk ran me off the road."

"So I see. Did you get a plate?" Rowley looked up and down the road and then leaned in her passenger window. "I did see a white pickup heading to town but I didn't take much notice. They're a dime a dozen around here."

Relieved to see a friendly face, Jenna nodded. "Yeah, I've noticed and, no, the plate had mud on it. I'm concerned it might have been the person watching me. Errol Dean maybe?"

"I doubt he'd tangle with you again." He narrowed his gaze. "He wouldn't be stupid enough—would he?"

Jenna shrugged. "Who knows for sure?" She pressed the starter again and nothing happened. "The truck is dead. Any suggestions?"

"It's a rental, isn't it?" Rowley smiled. "If you call them, I'll tow it out of the ditch. They'll send someone out to pick it up and drop off another rental."

Jenna collected her things and nodded. "Okay, and while we're waiting for them to arrive, can you drive me back to my ranch? I need to lock the gate. I left it wide open."

"Yes, ma'am." Rowley smothered a grin. "Left in kind of a hurry, huh?"

"Yeah, like my tail was on fire." She smiled and made the call.

After helping Rowley attach a tow rope to the truck and dragging it back onto the road, Jenna checked the time. "They said they'd send a tow truck within the hour and asked me to go back with him to the rental place at the airport to pick up another."

"I don't figure that's a good idea in the circumstances." Rowley headed back toward her ranch. "If this is someone out to get you for whatever reason, maybe you should consider this accident could be an elaborate setup to get you into the tow truck. Best I take you to the rental place, but why don't you consider using one of the cruisers? They're old, but they seem okay. The one I'm driving runs just fine."

Unsure of the local protocol, Jenna shrugged. "Yeah, but I'm not on duty twenty-four/seven, I can't possibly use a cruiser for personal use."

"Trust me." Rowley chuckled. "You're on duty twenty-four/seven, plus you're the sheriff. You make the rules."

Jenna raised her eyebrows. "Acting sheriff."

"That's not what is says on your jacket, ma'am. Wait here.

It's probably better if I shut the gate. No one is gunning for me." Rowley pulled up at her open gate, took a long look around, and then jumped out, swung it shut, and clicked the padlock.

Chewing on her bottom lip, Jenna searched the woods, looking into the surrounding land. Nothing glinted and only the beauty of Montana greeted her. She turned to Rowley as he slid back behind the wheel. "Thanks. I'm annoyed someone has spoiled this place for me. It's supposed to be my safe place, my forever home."

"It will be." Rowley backed out onto the blacktop and headed back to the highway. "You mentioned the security and alterations. I'm sure once they're completed, you'll feel safer. One thing, can you get an electronic gate? Stopping to open the gate could be dangerous, especially at night."

Nodding, Jenna sighed as they pulled up behind the damaged rental. "Yeah, I'm putting in security fencing, CCTV cameras, and a remote-control gate." She looked away, not wanting to mention the safe room in the barn. "I figure with a security system surrounding the house, I'll be warned if anyone breaks through. I don't like the idea of people sneaking up on me."

"Then add a sign." Rowley drummed his fingers on the steering wheel. "People around these parts don't usually walk onto a property posted with TRESPASSERS WILL BE SHOT signs." He grinned at her. "But you'll have to be awake early to allow the snowplow guy access to your driveway, being as you're alone and all, or come winter you'll be snowed in until the melt. He lives right next door."

Seeing the tow truck pull up, Jenna sighed with relief. "I'll be sure to make his acquaintance well before the first snow." She slid from the passenger seat. "I'll go and speak to the driver. We'll follow him out to the rental place. They'll want a report for their insurance."

"Yes, ma'am." Rowley tipped his hat.

TWENTY-ONE

The next couple of weeks went by without incident. What Jenna considered a problem at the time was just brushed aside by Deputy Walters, and when told about the accident on the highway, he made light of it by saying someone was just skylarking... whatever that meant. The paperwork on the ranch had come through at last, but she'd decided to remain in town during the alterations. Someone had spooked her and not being out there alone before the security went up was her best and safest option. Once the security was firmly in place and the furniture arranged, she'd move in and become one of the townsfolk. She'd been pleasantly surprised when Rowley had offered to go with her to oversee the alterations to the ranch. It was as if he understood her hesitation at driving out there alone. He had become a very helpful asset and treated her like his boss, which she appreciated, but in truth, having him around was like having a younger brother.

Each day she took one of the cruisers out on patrol with Rowley riding shotgun. They did their usual sweep of the town and detoured to the showgrounds to catch the preparation for a county fair and rodeo. People moved around the showgrounds, carrying saddles or moving horses and cattle. Cowboys leaned on corral fences, talking loud like a bunch of kids. People kept on looking at the sky. The festival was running late this year due to some freaky weather in other counties.

Jenna took her time, enjoying the Western feel, the smell of horses and leather. She asked Rowley a stream of questions and discovered the cowboys were holed up in trailers or had taken a bed in some of the bunkhouses around the grounds. Turning to Rowley, she pointed to a poster. "That guy is on all the posters. Is he the king of the rodeo or something?"

"That would be Walt Devers, last year's triple-crown champion." He smiled. "You'll be down here keeping the peace, so you'll get to see plenty of events."

Concerned, Jenna took in the scope of the place. It was huge. How could she possibly maintain peace with one old deputy and a rookie? She cleared her throat not wanting to make Rowley feel inadequate. "Did the previous sheriff manage all this alone?"

"Hell no." Rowley's face broke into a wide grin. "He called in deputies from Louan and Blackwater." He raised both eyebrows. "They're the two closest towns and have a ton of deputies. Louan has sapphire mines and the town council is the leaseholder. They made a good investment. The town is rich and they have deputies to spare. Blackwater has more than it needs as well. "I'll be happy to call them to assist. We'll need them for shifts over the weekend." He glanced at her. "We usually book rooms for them at the motel." His brow crinkled into a frown. "I hope they have vacancies. Many people stop over for the rodeo but many come in trailers." He sighed. "With us working as well, maybe eight would make life easier. The mayor picks up the tab. The rodeo is a big money spinner for the town."

Jenna turned and they headed back to the cruiser. "Okay,

I'll leave that to you. You should call Maggie to organize the accommodation and meals."

As Rowley made the calls, Jenna drove back to town. They'd just hit the end of Stanton when she spotted a curl of smoke climbing into the bright blue sky. "Oh, that doesn't look good. That's in the middle of town."

"I hope no one has set fire to the sheriff's office. I'll call Maggie back and put my phone on speaker." Rowley lifted his phone again. "Hey, Maggie, it's me again. Is everything okay there? We see smoke."

"I was just going to call you about that. There's a ton of smoke but the fire department has it under control." Maggie sounded her usual calm self. *"Walters just walked in. He told me it was the apartment on top of the hardware store. It went up with a whoosh. They found a body and we're waiting for a report from the fire chief."*

Dread crept over Jenna and she swallowed hard. "Did you say the hardware store?"

"Yes, that's what Walters said." Maggie sucked in a deep breath. *"Oh my Lord, isn't that where young Mrs. Dean was staying?"*

Jenna flicked a glance at Rowley's grim expression. "Tell Walters to hunt down Errol Dean. I want to know if he was involved."

"Ma'am." Walters slow drawl filled the speaker. *"Before you go hauling anyone in, do you figure you should talk to the fire chief? It could have been an accident. From what I hear, Errol Dean has been in counseling and was hoping to get back with his wife."* He sighed. *"Seems to me if his wife just died in a house-fire, hauling him downtown might be a little insensitive—seeing as you're going for sheriff and all."*

Having taken the brunt of Dean's temper firsthand, Jenna gritted her teeth. "Well, I don't trust him and I want to know where he was at the time of the fire. You don't have to haul him in. Go find him and see if he has an alibi. I'm on my way to the scene now."

She pulled up some ways from the smoking hardware store. The store itself appeared to be untouched by the fire but around the windows of the top floor, fire had left flaming patterns in soot on the red bricks. The air held the disturbing smell of a cookout, and knowing Carol Dean had burned to death inside made her stomach churn. The fire crew was in the process of mopping up, and paramedics stood leaning against an ambulance talking in hushed voices. A small crowd had gathered on the sidewalk opposite with all eyes on the building like a murder of crows waiting to feed on the dead.

Jenna turned to Rowley. "We'll need to process the scene. Have you seen a person killed in a fire before?"

"No, ma'am." Rowley appeared to steel himself and one hand rested on the door handle. "I'll be fine."

Handing him a mask and gloves from the kit in the cruiser, she slid out and headed for the fire chief. It took some minutes to gain his attention, and Jenna had the feeling he didn't want her to become involved. *Too bad.* She followed him to his truck. "Sorry to trouble you, Chief." She held out a hand. "Sheriff Jenna Alton. Can you walk me through the scene? Is the body in situ?"

"Yeah. Doc Brown has already come by and confirmed the woman is deceased. He'll be making out a death certificate." He ignored her hand. "It's nothing for you to worry about, Sheriff. It's cut and dried."

Straightening, Jenna frowned. "You may not know the circumstances surrounding Carol Dean, who we assume died in the fire, but any death warrants an investigation by my office." She stared into a bored expression. "Unless you have to rush to another fire, would you mind giving me a rundown of your conclusions?"

"Sure." The chief walked round back of the hardware store,

his boots splashing through the puddles of ash-filled water. "The stairs are fine. All the damage was contained to the bedroom. The structure of the building looks untouched, although the hardware store has suffered water damage, but I'm sure it can be repaired."

Getting more annoyed by the second. "I'm sure the insurance company will send out someone to do a structural inspection."

"That's my job." The chief narrowed his eyes at her. "I'm more than qualified to assess the damage to a building and make a conclusion on a fire, Sheriff."

Pulling on her mask and gloves, she indicated to Rowley to follow them up the stairs on the outside of the building. "Was the front door open when you arrived?"

"It obviously wasn't locked." The chief walked inside. "I can't see any damage, so my crew didn't have to break down the door." He led the way inside the bedroom.

The smell of burned wood, ashes, and a smoldering corpse crawled up Jenna's nose. She stared down at the small blackened figure curled up under the window and moved toward it. Although burned, a considerable gash was clearly visible on the forehead. Concerned, she looked at the chief. "So, what do you figure happened here?"

"I found an electrical fault in the wiring to the lamp. I'd say the cord ignited." He pointed to the outlet. "The fire spread to the rug. The woman panicked, tripped, struck her head on the bench, and knocked herself out. The open window fed the fire and she burned to death. I'll get the paramedics to come and take her to the undertakers."

"No, I'm not finished here." Jenna stared at the pattern of fire. "I see the burn marks come from the outlet and move to the lamp but why didn't the fire stop with the lamp? What made it jump to the rug and head toward the woman? The scorch marks lead to the front door, which you said was unlocked, but apart from a small amount of soot, the door hasn't been damaged." She bent to examine the Y-shaped pattern with interest. "Do you have an explanation for this?"

"Is she always so annoying?" The chief looked at Rowley and grinned.

Anger rising, Jenna shot a glance at Rowley as he opened his mouth to reply and he shut it with a disgruntled expression. She glared at the chief. "Are you always so rude?" She cleared her throat. "Okay, if the fire started at the outlet and moved as you reckon across the rug to the woman, why does it do a turn-around and head back to the front door?"

"Okay... let me explain this for you in words you'll under-stand." He walked to the outlet. "The fire starts here in the outlet and runs along the cord and then across the rug. The woman sees the fire and panics. She can't get past, so flings open the window looking for an escape but it's too late. The flames have caught hold of her skirt. She falls to the floor banging her head. The wind from the window blows the flames to the front door."

Heat crawled up Jenna's neck and into her cheeks. Not in all her career had anyone treated her like an idiot. She lifted her chin. "I'm not buying it. Have you checked for an accelerant?"

"Can you smell anything like gas or gunpowder? How many times do I have to explain to you? IT WAS AN ELEC-TRICAL FAULT." The chief shook his head. "Don't step on my toes, missy. I'll send in my report. When it comes to fires, I'm the expert in this town, not you." He turned, walked out the door, and clattered down the steps.

Holding back the need to scream, Jenna stared after him. "What a jerk."

TWENTY-TWO

Ignoring the fire chief's assessment of the scene, Jenna stared at the pattern of the fire. She'd never seen any like it before. Fire usually moved forward roughly in a line unless it followed some type of accelerant, either liquid or something else flammable, but the wooden floor was the same all over. So how come the fire branched off in two different directions? Confused, she went to the electrical outlet and turned to Rowley. "They haven't removed the outlet to check for a fault in the wiring. I don't like this at all. Do you have anything to remove the cover so we can check?" She went to the power box just to make sure the power was disconnected.

"Yeah, I do, ma'am, and the chief had no right to raise his voice at you like that. It was disrespectful." He pulled a penknife from his pocket and opened it, displaying a variety of tools. He crouched down and went to work removing the outlet.

Concentrating on what Rowley was doing, she snorted. "He was rude but I can take it. I've met worse men than him in my career." She looked at him. "I appreciate you wanting to say something, but no matter how much you feel like you need to protect me from men like him, don't step in and defend me.

Watch my back in a fight or when we're in danger, but it's best to allow me to deal with people like him." She sighed, not wanting to admonish Rowley. "I want to win the election for sheriff, and if you step in and defend me from people like him, it will soon get around that I'm weak."

"You're sure not weak." Rowley lifted out the wires and shook his head. "This wasn't a wiring fault. All the fire damage is to the outside." He straightened and frowned at her. "What now?"

Jenna pulled out her phone. "I'll record the scene. You go down to the cruiser and grab the forensics kit. I'll need samples of everything and I want someone other than the local undertaker examining the body." She turned to him. "Isn't there a doctor or anyone who can do an autopsy on the victim in town?"

"Doc Brown is an option, but he's just a GP. He's already seen the body, but he's not a forensic scientist. You'll have to contact the medical examiner's office in Helena. Most times the undertaker, Max Weems, handles any bodies and has done for years." Rowley headed for the door. "I'll be right back."

Jenna took shots of the outlet and the burn pattern on the floor and turned back to the charred body of Carol Dean. She took images from every angle and then used the video camera on her phone and gave a running commentary of everything she noticed as she captured the scene. When Rowley came back with the forensics kit, she smiled at him. "Remove the outlet and as much wiring as possible. Bag and tag everything—date, time—and we'll both sign the seal. I'm taking swabs of all the burned areas to look for any sign of an accelerant. I'm convinced this pattern of fire isn't normal. It's as if someone laid a trail of a flammable liquid and then set it alight."

"Why would they do that?" Rowley set about collecting evidence.

Jenna took a long look at the victim. "I figure someone

murdered Carol Dean and tried to make it look like an accident. When I'm done collecting samples, we're going over the entire apartment checking for prints. Then we're going to see if we can find a murder weapon because the blood on the nightstand looks smeared to me and I see spatter on the ceiling. That's impossible if she fell and hit her head, and looks to me like someone hit her more than once and the spatter came from the murder weapon when it was raised in an arc." She swung her arm up in the air to demonstrate.

"I can reach the ceiling." Rowley took a swab kit from the bag. "I'll collect samples from the spatter. You'll need to match it to Mrs. Dean to prove your theory."

Jenna smiled at him. "Okay, get at it. I'll call Maggie to get onto the medical examiner's office in Helena and she'll be able to give me the undertaker's number. We can store the body there for now." She pulled out her phone and made the call. When she'd disconnected, she called the local undertaker. "Max Weems? Hi, this is Sheriff Alton. I'm sending you a body. It could be a murder victim and I don't want it to be touched. Leave it in the body bag and keep it refrigerated. I'm waiting on advice from the medical examiner's office in Helena." She nodded to herself. "Thank you. I'll be in touch."

"What about notifying next of kin?" Rowley handed her an evidence bag to sign. "Does she have anyone in town?"

Jenna pulled out her notebook and flipped through the pages. "She mentioned her family was out of Grand Junction, Colorado. We'll need to chase them down." She smiled. "Now we have a reason to speak to Errol Dean. He'll have all the information we need. I'll call Walters and get him on it. I doubt he's spoken to him yet." She called Walters and explained. "Once you find her parents' location, have the local cops pay them a visit. They'll need a DNA sample from the mother, and any information we might need for a positive ID. The name of her dentist and physician would be good." She stared at the wall.

"Okay, get at it now, and call me the second you know anything." Disconnecting, she pushed the phone back inside her pocket.

After the paramedics removed the body, Jenna set about collecting evidence. As luck would have it, they had Errol Dean's fingerprints on record and, she doubted he'd visited Carol since the protective order was still in place—unless he'd killed her. They'd just about finished when Deputy Walters called. Jenna stared at the caller ID. She put the phone on speaker and pulled out her notebook. "What have you got for me?"

"Errol Dean was cooperative. He gave me all the information you wanted." Walters sounded uncomfortable. *"He broke down when I told him about his wife's death and wanted to go see her. It made questioning him difficult, but he says he was in town with his brother, Lou, before the fire was reported. He said at the time they were at Aunt Betty's Café. After, he went to the bank and noticed the fire department when he came out."*

Jenna made notes. "Where is Lou now? I want to speak to him."

"Lou is staying with him." Walters cleared his throat. *"They're both at home now but work nightshift at the meat-packing plant. I'll send you the address."*

"Thanks." Jenna disconnected, checked the crime scene once more, and then collected the evidence bags and handed them to Rowley. "There's no sign of a murder weapon. I'll check the dumpster before we leave. You head back to the cruiser and get the evidence into the containers. I'll close the door and seal it with crime scene tape."

"Do you figure Dean killed his wife and set the fire?" Rowley paused on the steps and looked back at her with his arms laden with bags.

Jenna nodded. "In murder following a spousal abuse case, the first person we look at is the husband. He had a motive. She was an ordinary person and as far as I can tell had no enemies. She was willing to stand up in court against him. That takes guts and also tells us she was terrified of him and wanted him locked away." She wrapped the crime scene tape around the steps from one side to the other handrail. "The evidence points to him and you should disregard the reaction to his wife's death. Most people are in shock and then break down. They don't carry on like that immediately. In my opinion, if he cared about her so much, he wouldn't have abused her." She shrugged. "He slapped me too. It came natural to him... too darn natural."

They found nothing in the dumpsters or during their search of the immediate area. Undeterred, Jenna climbed into the cruiser and put the coordinates for Dean's residence into the GPS. The old device was taking its time finding a signal and she glanced at Rowley. "I guess you know where Pine is?"

"Yeah, out near the college. Head through town and take Stanton. I'll show you where to turn." Rowley glanced at his watch. "When we drop by Aunt Betty's to validate their alibi, can we stop for a slice of pie? It's a long time until supper."

Jenna didn't need an excuse to drop by Aunt Betty's Café. The warm friendly atmosphere and amazing food had a magical charm, pulling in customers at an incredible rate. Being open from breakfast until the last customers left around eleven at night, seven days a week, was unusual for what was described as a small town to her, but she'd found herself in there for three meals a day. She drove through town and along Stanton. The highway, named after Stanton Forest, bordered the colossal expanse of dense pine trees that climbed the granite mountain ranges and nestled alongside Black Rock Falls, the wide and picturesque waterfall that fed the rivers and lakes all through Black Rock Falls County. In August the forest was alive with color, patches of wildflowers and shades of green and gold abounded, and the fresh fragrance born on the mountain air was enticing. Each time she drove close by, the need to stop and explore engulfed her with a longing. She glanced at Rowley. "When we get some downtime, can I borrow your mom's mare and take a ride in the forest?" She allowed the wind blowing in her window to ruffle her hair. "No wonder people come here for a vacation. It's so beautiful."

"You shouldn't go alone. It's easy to get lost in there. I'll have time over the weekend to take you to the res if you like. You must meet Atohi Blackhawk. He's the best tracker around these parts and a nice guy. Do you mind if we take Dana?" Rowley's neck pinked. "She's my girl and might take it the wrong way if she sees me out with you when we're not on duty."

Surprised that he might believe someone of her age would be a threat or that people might consider she'd break every rule in the book and seduce a rookie, Jenna smiled. "Heavens no. I'd love to meet her and I'll take that as a compliment. I'm about eight years your senior."

"Eight years?" Rowley's brows rose. "Oh, I figured you for about twenty-three." He pointed ahead. "Next turn on the right."

Jenna pulled the cruiser to the curb outside a log cabin. The garden had once been lovingly tended. Flowerbeds spilled over with blooms, but weeds had grown and the grass needed cutting. She headed to the front door and, using the flat of her hand, banged hard. The door flew open and Errol Dean glared down at her. For a man who'd just lost his beloved wife, his appearance was perfectly normal. She would have thought shedding a tear for Carol would have left his eyes red-rimmed.

"What the hell do you want?" Errol filled the door and soon another man, who from the likeness had to be his brother, Lou, joined him.

Jenna stood her ground. This man didn't frighten her. "I appreciate your cooperation with Deputy Walters earlier, but I'll need a statement from you and your brother concerning your whereabouts at the time Carol died." She waved her statement book at him. "May we come inside?"

"Ah—" Errol glanced at his brother and they exchanged whispers that Jenna couldn't hear.

"We can do this here or downtown? I need a statement one way or another." Jenna glanced from one angry face to the other. "You do realize, as Carol was under a protection order, the first person we look at is the husband. If you have a witness to prove where you were at the time of the fire, then I'll leave you alone."

"Okay." Errol stood to one side and Jenna walked into the hallway with Rowley close behind. The house was a mess and had the stench of a garbage truck.

She followed Errol and his brother into a kitchen with every surface piled high with takeout cartons, dirty dishes, and food wrappers. A loaf of bread covered with blue mold sat on the bench beside a rancid stick of butter. She pulled out her pen and, pushing a pile of plates to one side, rested the statement book on the kitchen table. "Okay, where were you when the fire broke out?"

"Eating in Aunt Betty's Café and after I went to the bank. It wasn't until I left there that I noticed the smoke." Errol frowned. "Lou was with me in the diner and they have CCTV. I have an ironclad alibi."

Wondering why an innocent man would even mention the cameras, Jenna wrote down what he'd said in the statement book. "Okay, add the approximate time you believe you were there and sign it." She offered him the book and turned to Lou. "Did you arrive at the same time as Errol?"

"Nope, a little after." Lou shrugged. "Don't look at me for this. I didn't even know where she lived until Deputy Walters showed before, so don't come to me with your accusations."

Startled by Lou's aggression, Jenna turned her attention back to Errol. "Did you know where Carol was living?"

"Yeah, but I didn't kill her." Errol rubbed the back of his neck. "I wanted her back."

Mind spinning, Jenna stared at him. She'd gone to great lengths to keep Carol's whereabouts secret. "How did you find out where Carol was living?"

"It was on the protection-order paperwork." Errol shrugged. "It states I'm not to go within ten yards of her or her residence." He handed back the statement book.

Angry at the incompetence of the clerk who issued the order, Jenna filled out the details for Lou Dean and handed the statement book to him. "Read this, add the time you arrived at Aunt Betty's, the time you left, and sign it." She turned back to Errol. "So, we won't find your fingerprints at Carol's apartment, is that right? You never went there?"

"Nope." Errol shuffled his feet. "Am I responsible for burying her? I'm barely keeping a roof over my head." He lifted his gaze to her. "She didn't have life insurance."

Disgusted, Jenna stared at him. "It seems fighting the divorce has come to bite you in the ass. Until it's final, you're Carol's next of kin and responsible for her remains." She pulled an evidence bag from her pocket and held it out to Lou. "If you'd drop the statement book and pen in here for me, please Mr. Dean."

"What the hell for?" Lou eyeballed her. "What's your game?"

Jenna wrinkled her nose. "Your hands are filthy and I'm a germaphobe." She looked around the kitchen in disgust. "This place needs to be condemned. I suggest you clean it up before I inform the town council. It's a health hazard."

To her surprise he dropped the book and pen into the bag. Jenna sealed it and met his confused gaze. His brother just stared at them openmouthed. "Thank you. We'll see ourselves out." She gave Rowley a meaningful look and they hurried out the door.

"That was pretty slick, ma'am." Rowley dropped into the seat beside her. "I wondered why you used a new statement book and ran the scanner over it before we left. You wanted to collect Lou's prints, right?"

Jenna started the engine and nodded. "Yeah, it's an old trick." She smiled at him. "I'll drop the evidence at the office and get Maggie to send the samples to the lab. I sure wish we had a medical examiner in town. It would make life so much easier."

"There's not too much for them to do around here." Rowley chuckled. "Accidents and old age are the main causes of death. Nothing bad happens in Black Rock Falls. Not now, anyway. There are rumors, and Atohi will tell you all kinds of stories about the forest, but I figure the worst that's happened is when people go missing it's because they fall into the ravine or the bears get them."

Jenna peered into the dense forest and the dark mysterious interior. As the afternoon sun dropped in the sky the long shadows looked foreboding and as the wind moved the branches anything, man or beast could be in there, hiding. She shook her head. "Well, if I was a serial killer and wanted to hide off the grid, Stanton Forest would be perfect." She raised both eyebrows. "They could be out there right now, just waiting for someone to walk on by."

TWENTY-THREE

After viewing the CCTV footage at Aunt Betty's Café, they discovered the Dean brothers had been in the café at the time of the fire. Errol had arrived first, and Lou about ten minutes later. As Jenna had no time of death nor could she get any more information from the fire chief on his estimate of when the fire started, she was at an impasse. She thanked Susie Hartwig, the assistant manager, and after ordering a meal, headed back to the table reserved for the sheriff's department, at the back but with a window close by. Beside her, Rowley got to his feet and hurried back to the counter. She watched with interest as he spoke to a very striking Native American man and then ushered him to their table.

"Sheriff, this is Atohi Blackhawk, the good friend I mentioned earlier." Rowley pushed the man forward.

Mesmerized by Atohi's expressive eyes and handsome features, Jenna stood and offered her hand. "Nice to meet you, Atohi. I feel I already know you. Jake speaks very highly of you."

"Ha, we have known each other for many years." Atohi sat down. "We have a similar interest in horses and the preservation of the forest." He smiled. "It is good to see a dedicated sheriff in town. Jake speaks highly of you too." He glanced at Rowley. "You should bring Sheriff Alton to the res and introduce her to my father. He would like to meet her." He looked at Jenna. "It will be good for the town to have a sheriff who cares. Our tribal elders will have much to discuss with you. Tribal law aside, we both have a mutual interest in the forest and rivers."

Jenna smiled. "We sure do. I'm looking forward to visiting the res and speaking with your father. It will be a great honor to speak with your elders. We have a case right now, but we'll be making plans as soon as possible... and please call me Jenna."

"Ah yes, the fire." Atohi frowned. "I would think it would be very unusual to have an electrical fault in the hardware store. The owner is an electrician and wired the entire place himself only recently. He had to make sure everything was up to code before he rented the apartment." He looked at Jenna. "I know this to be true because he told me when I dropped by a couple of months ago."

"We think it was deliberate." Rowley dropped his voice to just above a whisper. "The wires have no signs of fire damage; everything is outside the outlet."

Jenna wondered why Rowley was divulging intricacies of the case with Atohi and raised her eyebrows at him in question. "Ah... we'll wait for the fire chief's report before we speculate."

"I see that discussing the case with me is of concern, Jenna." Atohi smiled at her. "I've worked with law enforcement all over, for some years now. I understand what we discuss never leaves the department. You can trust me. My only interest here is solving a possible crime... and I believe I have valuable knowledge to contribute." He met her gaze. "I know fire. I've lived surrounded by the forest all my life. Knowing how fire moves is part of survival. If you have doubts an electrical fault caused this fire, then someone committed murder."

Jenna caught Rowley's nod of approval and leaned closer to

Atohi, but she doubted anyone had overheard them. "I believe Carol was dead before the fire started, and from what I can see, whoever killed her used an accelerant to spread the fire. The fire chief says it's an open-and-shut case of an electrical fault." She gave him her suspicion of the use of the accelerant and the fire pattern.

"So, someone struck and killed her and then set the scene to make it look like an accident." Atohi stroked his chin and thought for some moments. "And yet you didn't smell gasoline?"

"Nope." Rowley shook his head. "And I got down close to the carpet and took samples."

"Can I go, see?" Atohi leaned back in his chair. "If the accelerant was poured from a can like this"—he leaned forward and poured salt into his hand and allowed it to pour from his palm onto the tablecloth—"it splashes some and the fire would jump in spot fires to the splashes. The fumes alone would ignite the splashes. If someone squirted it, like from a bottle of lighter fuel or rubbing alcohol, it would be in a thin line enough to ignite but more controlled." He collected all the salt from the table and dropped it onto a plate. "That would make it less likely for them to catch their clothes on fire when lighting the accelerant too." He stared at Jenna. "Both scenarios are dangerous. It would be drop a match and run. Not bend down and ignite the fuel with a lighter."

Jenna nodded. "Okay, when we're finished up here. Come and take a look. I'd value your opinion. Not that any of our opinions will matter. There will be no case to answer if the fire chief rules it as an electrical fault. I'll have to go over his head and hope the medical examiner from Helena agrees to oversee the case." She sipped her coffee and sighed. "We need our own medical examiner in town. I wonder how many crimes have occurred here and been overlooked because of lack of a forensic team."

"Many." Atohi let out a long sigh. "Hunters find bones, and

before you arrived, all were assumed to be ancient burial sites." He snorted. "We know where our people are buried but no one asks us. The sheriffs before you believed they knew best. I know you're different, Jenna. I can see the warrior spirit in your eyes. You'll fight for the truth."

After finishing their meal, they went back to Carol Dean's gutted apartment. Below in the hardware store, the owner had a team of people loading stock into trucks. From what she could see, the damage to the store was substantial. It had water damage and the owner would need to replace part of the ceiling. She spoke briefly with him and discovered he'd be moving to a vacant store he owned opposite the real estate office on Main. The disruption to his business would only be a day or so. The current building, he'd already made plans to sell to a company wanting to build an outdoors store. She blinked. For a sleepy town, things sure moved fast in Black Rock Falls.

She leaned against the wall as Atohi examined the fire pattern across the floor, and when he remarked at a tiny patch of soot, she bent to look closer. "What do you see?"

"When a match burns fast, it curls." Atohi pointed to a tiny patch of soot. "That would be carbon from a matchstick. I believe they used alcohol. They squirted it from the victim to the lamp, the lamp to the outlet, then the person soaked the body and made a trail from the body to the door. They threw in a match, using the front door for protection. Alcohol burns cleaner than gasoline, so it would be easily missed. There's no smell once it's ignited. There wouldn't have been much initial smoke and the killer had time to walk away before anyone noticed. Another thing is, see how the newspapers are stacked close to where the body lay? He likely soaked them as well. See how small pieces of newsprint are over the floor like ash?"

Jenna pulled out her phone and took pictures of everything and then carefully gathered samples. "All this could be evidence in a murder case, but the main suspect was in Aunt Betty's Café at the time of the fire."

"He had time to get there before anyone noticed the fire. You'll need a professional to prove it. Maybe call in a fire expert from another town." Atohi's brow wrinkled and he turned to look at the lamp. "Hmm, even more evidence. The lamp switch is in the off position. It was daytime. Why would the victim need a light on? So how could the outlet cause a fire?"

"I'll take photographs of the lamp." Rowley grinned at Jenna. "Didn't I tell you Atohi would help us?"

Allowing all Atohi's amazing observations to filter through her mind, Jenna nodded. "Yeah, you sure did." She smiled at Atohi. "I appreciate your observations. If I can get a medical examiner's team from Helena, they'll do a forensics sweep. I'm convinced this was a homicide."

TWENTY-FOUR

It had been a long day of chasing shadows. The most compelling evidence was seeing Errol Dean standing on the corner staring up at the apartment. He'd stopped Jenna on the way to the cruiser and demanded to know what had happened to his wife. It was a ploy she'd seen before from a guilty man. Many returned to the scene of the crime to relive the moment. Jenna ignored his questions, saying she had no information to give him and was waiting on a report from the fire chief, which was true. The fact she had evidence to prove a homicide played on her mind. She made a call to the DA. The man was reasonable and listened to what she had to say: "I'd like you to wait until I can at least get a reply from the Helena medical examiner's office. They'll be looking at the evidence I've forwarded them and then deciding if they want to be involved."

"The fire chief is usually the go-to expert on fires, Sheriff." He cleared his throat. *"Going over his head seems a little unnecessary, as his assessment of the scene indicates an electrical fault caused the fire. Have you spoken to the mayor about this request?"*

Annoyed Jenna, checked the time, picked up her things,

and headed out the office. She locked the door and headed to her cruiser. "I'm the acting sheriff and the evidence I've found is well within the guidelines of requesting a medical examiner to investigate a probable homicide. I'll speak to the mayor if you insist, but in the meantime, I'll send you copies of the evidence we've collected." She sucked in a deep breath. "I figure the medical examiner's office will want to investigate the case."

"Okay, I'll look over it." He disconnected.

She drove the short way to the house she'd rented and went inside. Exhausted from a long day, she headed straight for the shower. After eating a reheated bowl of chili from Aunt Betty's Café, she brushed her teeth and fell into bed. Asleep in seconds, she slept like the dead until the click of a lock shot her awake and soft footsteps scuffled away. Every hair on her body stood to attention with the knowledge someone was in the house. The pungent smell of rubbing alcohol filled her nostrils and her eyes watered. Had Carol's killer gotten inside and was trying to burn her alive as well? Fully alert, she stared around in the gloom. Her bedroom door was now closed and she'd left it open. *Why would they do that?*

She listened intently. The old floorboards in the hallway creaked as someone moved around, no doubt setting up the scene to resemble another electrical fault. Heart pounding, she reached for her Glock on the bedside table and ran her palm over the bedclothes, feeling the evaporating chill of rubbing alcohol. Fluid soaked through the covers and the legs of her PJ's. If Carol's killer was in the house and struck a match she'd go up in flames. Panic gripped her and, laying down her weapon, she leaped from the bed, stripped off her PJ's and tossed them onto the bed. In silent steps she eased across the floor and grabbed the clothes she'd set out for the morning. Dressing at light speed, she pulled on her boots, strapped on her duty belt, and holstered her weapon. Her Glock was useless. A gunshot would ignite the fumes. She had to think fast—think like the killer. She had a chance to escape if he used the same technique to start the fire.

The creak of floorboards came closer this time. Hairs prickled on the back of her neck as she glanced around frantically looking for a way to escape. She'd never fit through the narrow windows in her room. The front door was her only way out. If the killer planned to ignite the accelerant, he wouldn't want anyone to see him and would leave by the back door.

Moving in silence, she pressed her back to the wall and froze, holding her breath as the handle to the door made a slight squeaking sound as the knob turned. Fear gripped her as the door slowly swung open, pinning her behind it. The smell of rubbing alcohol hit her in a wall of fumes as a black shape backed away from the room squirting a path of fluid on the floor. She trembled as realization hit her. He'd come back to open her door to ensure she'd burn to death. With such dense fumes, once ignited there'd be no escape. She had to act now before he struck the match.

As the person backed into the kitchen and out of sight, Jenna slid out in the pitch dark and moving like a shadow made her way to the front door. Holding her breath, she turned the key in the lock and pulled on the handle. A gust of wind from the open door swept through the house, and a bright light exploded in the kitchen, forcing her out the door and onto her knees. An ear-piercing scream cut the silence as the house ignited in a woosh.

Mesmerized by the speed of the dancing flames, Jenna turned to stare through the door at the path of fire running across the floor. An instant later a fireball burst from her bedroom in a roar. Heat brushed her exposed flesh as she rolled on the ground. Winded, she staggered to her feet and ran to her cruiser. Diving behind it she hit the blacktop gasping for breath. Flames reached out, igniting the grass, and an explosion rose up in a mushroom of destruction, shaking the ground and rocking the vehicle. Hit by a wall of heat, Jenna covered her face. Debris rained down on her and, trembling so hard her teeth chattered, she rolled under the cruiser. Fumes from the inferno suffocated her. Dazed and disorientated, she holed up under the greasy, dusty cruiser as the crackling house singing its death song succumbed to the flames.

"Jenna." A strong hand had her by the arm. "Come with me. It's not safe here."

She turned to see Atohi, kneeling beside the cruiser with bits of flaming wood scattered around him. "Okay." She rolled out and he pulled her to her feet, dragging her away at a run toward his truck.

"Are you hurt?" Atohi opened his truck door. "Get inside. It's safer."

"I think I'm okay." Breathless, she climbed inside and stared at him. "What are you doing here?"

"I work out with Jake every morning at the dojo." He cracked open a bottle of water and handed it to her. "I meet him there at five." He glanced at his watch. "I figure I'm going to be late this morning." He indicated to the house. "Did you forget to turn off the stove?"

Jenna shook her head. "No, someone was planning on burning me alive. They snuck into my bedroom when I was asleep and doused the bed in rubbing alcohol. When he closed my bedroom door, he woke me."

"Seems to me you're lucky he didn't cave in your head." Atohi's eyes narrowed. "So how did you make it out?"

Staring at the flames rising against a still dark morning sky, Jenna sipped the water. In the distance she could hear the firetrucks wailing their arrival. She turned back to him, holding tight to the bottle to stop her hands trembling. "I could hear him moving around. I figured he was setting up the house to make it look like an accident. Same as he did with Carol Dean. I had time to strip off the wet clothes and dress. I'd have confronted him. I had my Glock, but firing in a cloud of fumes would've been suicide. I knew he'd open my door to allow the fire to get to me and would probably use the back door to ignite the accelerant, so I waited. When he came back to open my door so I'd burn to death, I slipped out. I headed for the front door, and must have opened it just as he set the alcohol alight. From the screams, I figure the wind from the front door blew the fire on him. I took off and dived behind my cruiser. No one came running out. He's probably still in there. You know the rest."

"Did you recognize him?" Atohi pulled a blanket from the back seat and wrapped it around her.

"Thanks." Jenna shook her head. "No, it was very dark inside and I hid behind the door." She rubbed her forehead to ease the ache. "I'm just lucky he didn't toss a match inside my room." She checked her pockets. Her wallet was inside her coat pocket along with her phone and car keys. "I'll call Rowley."

"No need." Atohi indicated with his chin to Rowley's truck moving past the firetruck. "I'm sorry you lost all your things. It looks like you'll be moving into the ranch earlier than planned."

Unable to take her gaze from the billowing steam pouring from the embers as water from the firetruck's hoses poured down on the fires, Jenna nodded. "I guess I have no choice. I've only lost a few changes of clothes. The cruiser doesn't look too damaged and my bags are inside. I was planning on moving as soon as the security perimeter is up and running, but the changes I've made to the house are finished. It has a good security system so I'll be fine."

"What the hell happened here?" Rowley opened the door and stared at them. "Don't tell me you've been targeted?"

"It sure looks that way." Atohi grimaced. "Jenna got out just before it blew sky high. I figure a gas tank went up. Just as well it was a small one or it would have taken out the whole block."

"You sure you're, okay?" Rowley's gaze ran over her. "You're sheet white under the soot."

"I'm fine." Jenna ignored the headache from hell and slid out of the seat. She handed Atohi the blanket. "The fire crew are going in and I want to see if there's a body in there." She glanced up at Rowley. "Whoever did this was burned up in the fire. I heard them scream."

She stood on shaky knees and leaned against the truck, noticing the dirt on her hands, the singed bits on the arms of her jacket, and the burned holes in the fabric. She swallowed hard, seeing her reflection in the truck's window. The fire had singed her hair and soot smeared her face in lines. Dust coated her from head to boots. "Let's go round back and see if they found anyone and then I'll go by the office and take a shower."

Walking beside Rowley, she waited for the paramedics to pull up to the curb before stepping with care through the hot water streaming from the blackened shell of the house. The fire chief stood to one side, and she picked her way to him. "Is it safe to go round back?"

"Yeah, but there's a body. I guess you knew that already, huh?" The fire chief shrugged. "From what I can see, you had an electrical fault, just like the other case. Shame your friend didn't make it out in time. The gas bottle exploded causing the majority of the damage. Can you give me a blow by blow of what happened before the fire occurred?"

Jenna gave him a direct stare. "I'll make sure you have a copy of my report."

She found the body outside the vicinity of the back door. A gaping hole had rendered the house unrecognizable and the burned figure on the ground likewise. A blackened mass replaced what should have been his face, she pushed her hands in her jacket pockets and found latex gloves. She handed Rowley a pair and pulled on her own. "Roll him over, I want to see if he's carrying any ID."

"I'm not good at this." Rowley gagged and walked away to

spew in the flowerbed. He came back and shrugged apologetically. "Sorry."

Jenna smiled at him. "We all do it at one time. Being a cop doesn't mean you're not human. Just help me roll him on his left side." She ran her hand over the untouched back of the man and found a wallet in his pants pocket. She flipped it open. "Lou Dean. I hadn't even considered him." She folded the wallet and straightened. "He arrived at Aunt Betty's Café ten minutes after his brother Errol, the day Carol died. That would have given Lou time to kill Carol, set the scene, and then hightail it to Aunt Betty's Café before anyone noticed the smoke. I guess we'll never be able to prove if they planned it together. Errol had an ironclad alibi by being at Aunt Betty's well before the fire." She shook her head. "Lou must have believed I'd found evidence against him after we collected his prints and figured by killing me, he'd walk. The idiot didn't have a brain in his head. Did he really reckon anyone would believe two fires from electrical faults in the same week would fly?"

"Well, he did mix it up a bit." Rowley rubbed his chin. "He didn't knock you out before he set fire to the house." He stared at the smoking ruins. "How did he get inside?"

Jenna shrugged. "As we don't have a door, I guess we'll never know. I doubt he forced the lock or he'd have woken me. He did that by shutting my bedroom door. He must have had a key. This place has been a rental for twenty years. Anything is possible." She pulled out her phone and took photographs of the scene and then waved at the paramedics to collect the body. "Take it straight to the undertaker. Tell Mr. Weems to keep him on ice until I talk to him."

She walked back to her cruiser. It was a little more damaged than she'd imagined, and Rowley had to pry open the trunk for her to collect her bags. "I hope the insurance covers the damage."

"You should ask for a new one." Rowley headed for his

truck. "That's one case solved... well, I figure two. Lou Dean was in the right place at the right time for Carol's murder and now this."

Jenna nodded. "It was probably Lou who caused the accident on the highway. That was a warning. This was attempted murder." She leaned against Rowley's truck and used her phone to run Lou Dean's name against the vehicle registration of owners of white trucks in town. She also ran his prints against the ones they'd collected at Carol's apartment.

As they waited, she thanked Atohi for his help and Rowley drove her to the office. Jenna took a shower and changed. Sometime later, the search gave up its results. Lou Dean did own a white truck and the fingerprints they'd collected at the scene of Carol Dean's murder matched as well. The call she'd made to the meat-processing plant, Errol Dean's workplace, confirmed he'd been there at the time of the fire at her house. "Errol Dean is going to walk on both counts. I'll never prove he was involved, although it sure looks suspicious." She looked at Rowley. "Write it up and we'll send a report to the medical examiner. With the evidence we've collected and my firsthand testimony of what happened to me, he'll call an inquest into Carol Dean's death, and the death of Lou Dean. It's normal procedure." She glanced at her watch. "I'll go write my statement, and when you're done, we're heading down to Aunt Betty's for breakfast."

"Yes, ma'am." Rowley grinned and touched his hat. "After what happened this week, no one will stand against you for sheriff. I figure you've proved you're the person to take care of Black Rock Falls."

Jenna smiled at him. "Are you sure?"

"Oh yeah." Rowley dropped into his chair. "It will be a privilege working beside you."

EPILOGUE

NOW

Relieved to have found the courage to tell Kane what had happened to her, Jenna had talked late into the morning. The story had continued through breakfast and during their chores. With Kane encouraging her to keep going, she'd divulged every last detail. She yawned as the lack of sleep caught up with her in a rush and dropped onto the sofa beside him. "The medical examiner commended me during the inquest and the fire chief was fired for incompetence."

"What about Errol Dean?" Kane rubbed his chin. "His name hasn't come up since I've been in town."

Recalling the scene, Jenna swallowed hard. "He took his own life in a motel room the day the inquest findings came down. I still don't know why Lou killed Carol, but the deaths of Errol's wife and brother pushed him over the edge."

"And the elections?" Kane met her gaze. "Did you have the townsfolk behind you?"

Jenna smiled. "I sure did." She chuckled. "I was very emotional and my knees shook like crazy when I stood up in front of everyone to be sworn in officially." She shrugged. "It was suddenly real. Part of me wanted to punch the air in triumph, but the other part was screaming at me that I wasn't ready to protect so many people. My first requisition to the town council was for more deputies and some decent cruisers." She laughed. "You have no idea how excited I was when your application for deputy sheriff arrived. I couldn't believe my luck. Finding someone with your experience was a gift." She grinned. "Then when you showed up wearing your combat face, I thought for sure the cartel had sent you to kill me."

"I didn't know what I'd walked into either. First you stuck a gun in my face and then I discovered my cottage was under CCTV surveillance." Kane shook his head. "You weren't what I expected, that was for darn sure."

She looked up at Kane, his face unreadable. Her stomach gave a little twist. How did he feel about her now? She'd had to tell him the truth about her past. It was the right thing to do. "I wanted to tell you about my relationship with Michael Carlos— not that I had any feelings for him at all, apart from disgust. Marrying him was necessary to get inside the cartel."

"You didn't have to tell me, but I'm sure glad you did, Jenna." Kane pulled her close. "You went to hell and back. I wish I'd been there to take him down."

Jenna shook her head. "The DEA tried everything to get inside the cartel and failed. Good men died, but they didn't suspect me... well, maybe toward the end Michael was starting to get suspicious. Well, now you know everything about me— the good and the bad."

"It sure explains why you're so passionate about spousal abuse and the PTSD episodes. I'm surprised you could function at all after living that hell." Kane stroked her cheek. "I can't imagine what you went through to bring him down. You're one determined woman, Jenna. I've never met anyone quite like you."

Jenna sighed. "Trust me, Michael made my skin crawl and being married to him, even if it was a sham marriage, disgusted me. I felt as if I'd lost another piece of my soul every time I was with him."

"I can't believe the DEA expected you to marry him." Kane shook his head slowly. "He was a psychopath. We had him down for murdering over thirty people. You told me about giving evidence against Viktor Carlos, but your actual mission was need to know. At the time, I never knew your name." He pulled her onto his lap. "It must have been a nightmare trapped with that animal for over two years. I doubt many people would have made it out alive. You're special, Jenna, real special. I figure only you could have singlehandedly destroyed the cartel and saved all those kids alone. They should have given you a medal."

Jenna snuggled against him. "We've both suffered to make the world a better place, Dave. It's what we signed up for. It was part of the job."

"Yeah, but I didn't have to sleep with someone or be abused constantly." Kane turned to look at her. "What he did to you is unforgivable. You should have bailed."

"I couldn't." Jenna shook her head. "Too many lives were at stake, and when I found out about the kids, I had to bring him down or die trying."

Concerned by the shudder that went through his body, she turned to look at him. "Does it make any difference, between us? Is it a problem that I was with Michael Carlos?"

"Is it a problem I was a government assassin?" Kane took both of her hands and looked into her eyes. "The truth now. Has it ever made a difference to how you look at me?"

Eyes misting, Jenna shook her head. "No, you're the kindest, gentlest man I've ever met. You have a heart as big as an elephant. I don't care what you did before you arrived in Black Rock Falls. I'm only interested in what I see right now."

"Exactly. I *know* you, Jenna. *My* Jenna, not DEA Agent Avril Parker. Let's agree to forget the past." Kane's expression softened. "We've been given a second chance. Whatever happens from now on, we'll face it together." He eased her from his lap, stood, and pulled her to her feet. "It's lunchtime. Let's eat and then go for a ride and enjoy the sunshine. Duke would love a run in the forest." He scrubbed his bloodhound's long floppy ears. "It promises to be a beautiful day and we have all afternoon to ourselves."

Jenna snorted. "There you go again, tempting fate. I figure we won't make it through to supper before someone calls nine one one."

"Ah, well." Kane squeezed her hand. "You can't say life is ever boring around here." He chuckled. "Although, I figure the town sign should read WELCOME TO BLACK ROCK FALLS— ENTER AT YOUR OWN RISK."

A LETTER FROM D.K. HOOD

Dear Reader,

Thank so much for choosing my novel and coming with me on the thrilling adventure of Jenna Alton's origin story in *Don't Look Back*. If you'd like to keep up to date with all my latest releases, just sign up at the website link below. Your email will never be shared and you can unsubscribe at any time.

www.bookouture.com/dk-hood

Writing this story has been quite an experience. Delving into the world of the drug cartel and undercover FBI agents was a new experience for me.

If you enjoyed my story, I would be very grateful if you could leave a review and recommend my book to your friends and family. I really enjoy hearing from readers, so feel free to ask me questions at any time. You can get in touch on my Facebook page or Twitter or through my blog.

Thank you so much for your support.

D.K. Hood

KEEP IN TOUCH WITH D.K. HOOD

http://www.dkhood.com
dkhood-author.blogspot.com.au

 facebook.com/dkhoodauthor
twitter.com/DKHood_Author

ACKNOWLEDGMENTS

Thank you so much to my wonderful editor, Helen, and Team Bookouture for giving me the opportunity to write Sheriff Jenna Alton's story. The strength of Jenna's character in the Kane and Alton series is my tribute to every woman who has battled against the odds to succeed.

I must thank the readers who took the time to post great reviews of my book and to those people who hosted me on their blogs.

Not to forget the amazing publicity and marketing teams at Bookouture—Noelle, you are a legend.

Also, a special and heartfelt thanks to Patricia Rodrigues, whose incredible talent brings my characters to life in the series of audiobooks.

Made in the USA
Monee, IL
12 February 2023

27666789R00090